Sam s...........n, his mouth pr........................bing hers. What................. dimly remembered ....ised himself he wouldn't rise to her bait, but she tasted too delectable to think about anything else.

He heard a gasp. *Guess she's way into this too.* Sam couldn't help feeling flattered. After all, he hadn't kissed anyone but Elizabeth for months, and it was nice to know that he hadn't lost his touch just because he had a girlfriend.

"Sam!"

Sam frowned as the kiss deepened. That was weird. How could Cathy kiss him *and* talk at the same time? Was she a ventriloquist? Not only that, but she managed to sound just like Jessica, too.

Jessica! Sam pulled away from Cathy in shock. He turned to see Jessica staring at him. She looked even more shocked than he did, and her face was turning an interesting shade of bright purple.

"Oh, man." Sam buried his head in his hands. "Oh, man."

Bantam Books in the Sweet Valley University series.
Ask your bookseller for the books you have missed.

And don't miss these Sweet Valley
University Thriller Editions:

Visit the Official Sweet Valley Web Site on the Internet at:

http://www.sweetvalley.com

SWEET VALLEY UNIVERSITY®

Super Edition

Face It

Written by
Laurie John

Created by
FRANCINE PASCAL

BANTAM BOOKS
NEW YORK · TORONTO · LONDON · SYDNEY · AUCKLAND

RL: 8, AGES 014 AND UP

FACE IT

A Bantam Book / August 2000

Sweet Valley High® and Sweet Valley University®
are registered trademarks of Francine Pascal.
Conceived by Francine Pascal.

Produced by 17th Street Productions,
an Alloy Online, Inc. company.
33 West 17th Street
New York, NY 10011.

ISBN: 0-553-49348-5

Visit us on the Web! www.randomhouse.com/teens

Published simultaneously in the United States and Canada

Bantam Books is an imprint of Random House Children's Books, a
division of Random House, Inc. BANTAM BOOKS and the rooster
colophon are registered trademarks of Random House, Inc. Bantam Books,
1540 Broadway, New York, New York 10036.

PRINTED IN THE UNITED STATES OF AMERICA

OPM   0 9 8 7 6 5 4 3 2 1

To Lilliana Cama

Chapter One

Dump him! He's a slacker! He's beneath you! Jessica Wakefield mentally yelled to her sister, Elizabeth.

Wasn't there such a thing as telepathy? Weren't twins supposed to have some kind of special connection? Obviously not. Because Elizabeth still sat at the kitchen table, a dreamy smile on her face, as she spooned some strawberry yogurt into her boyfriend Sam's lying, cheating mouth.

Can I throw up now? Jessica thought as she yanked open the refrigerator door. Since when had Elizabeth Wakefield become the type of girl who spoon-fed her boyfriend? For almost a year now, ever since Sam had moved into the off-campus house with her, Elizabeth, and Neil Martin at the start of their sophomore year, Elizabeth had kept Sam at arm's length. The guy's very presence had irritated her sister. And then last week Sam and

1

Elizabeth had hooked up into couplehood. Despite *everything* he'd put her through!

"Hey! Where's the half gallon of skim milk I bought yesterday?" Jessica demanded, slamming the door shut.

Sam Burgess glanced up at her. "You mean that watery stuff? I think I used the last of it. It was pretty rank, so be glad there's none left."

Can I kill him? Jessica wondered. *Oh, that's right, why should I bother? His very own live-in cheerleader and protector would have me arrested before I even got my hands around his loser neck!*

"The point is, *Sam*," Jessica fumed, "the skim milk was mine. Which should have meant *you* don't use it. Get it?"

"Um, Jess," Elizabeth cut in. "I'm the one who used most of it. I had a cereal attack last night. Sorry."

Ha! Jessica thought bitterly. *Like Elizabeth would ever use something of someone else's! Who is she trying to kid? She's just covering up for her inconsiderate, lying slacker of a boyfriend!*

Jessica still couldn't get over the fact that her overachieving twin sister was going out with Sam, whose only goal in life was a free ride. *What does she see in him?* Jessica asked herself for the hundredth time. At first she'd thought that the Elizabeth-and-Sam thing was just a passing fad. Her superstraight sister was working through a bad-boy phase, that was all. Jessica could totally hang with that; she'd had quite a few bad-boy phases herself. But this one didn't seem to be passing—in fact, as the days went by, Elizabeth and Sam seemed to be even tighter.

"Hey, has anyone seen my poli-sci notes?" Neil Martin asked frantically as he pushed through the swinging door of the kitchen. Neil was Jessica's best friend. He was also the guy of her dreams. Well, he *would* be if he weren't gay. A worried frown distorted Neil's gorgeous face. "I'm desperate. The final's in a couple of hours, and I'm clueless about when Austria invaded Germany."

"It was the other way around," Sam said. "Germany invaded Austria."

Neil opened the refrigerator and pulled out a carton of orange juice. He turned to Sam. "Hey, I thought OCC was a community college for those who couldn't hack it at SVU. But you guys actually learn over there."

"You're a riot," Sam replied.

"Actually, Neil," Elizabeth said, "Sam's just really smart." She smiled at her boyfriend.

Jessica rolled her eyes. Sam went to Orange County College because he *couldn't* get into Sweet Valley University.

Neil poured himself a glass of OJ. "Where did I

3

put those notes? I have to find them, or I'm dead. Unless you want to take the final for me, Burgess."

"I'd help you out, buddy," Sam said, "but I've got my own finals."

Jessica yanked her English muffin out of the toaster, then sat down at the table across from Elizabeth and Sam. *Yeah, like International Beer 101 and Playstation for College Students,* she thought snidely. "I think I saw your poli-sci notes on the couch, Neil."

Neil gave her a big, wet kiss on the cheek, then rushed out of the kitchen. "You're a genius!" he announced as he barged back in, waving the notes over his head. He grabbed a chair and straddled it backward, then took a bite out of Jessica's muffin. "Can I have this half? I'm starving and have zero time to make anything."

"No prob." Jessica knew the kind of pressure that Neil was under; after all, she had only finished with her own finals the day before. And for the first time in her life, she'd actually stressed over them. Interestingly, there had been something kind of fun about pulling all-nighters in the library and getting into studying the way she'd always seen Elizabeth do.

She glanced at her sister, who was proofreading a take-home final. "Wow, that thing goes on forever."

"I know," Elizabeth murmured. "But I really

4

want an A. There! I'm done!" She dropped her pen and massaged her hand.

"Guess where I'm going today?" Jessica said.

"Shopping?" Sam asked.

As Elizabeth nudged Sam in the ribs, Jessica shot him a dirty look. "For your information, Sam, I happen to be going to a very important gallery in Sweet Valley to discuss the possibility of a summer internship."

Elizabeth's mouth dropped open. "Wow, Jess, that's great!"

"What did you line up?" Jessica asked her, sure that her sister had scored a very serious summer job as a journalist on a local newspaper. That would be cool. Elizabeth would definitely meet a hot writer type who'd steal her away from undeserving Sam.

"Nothing yet," Elizabeth said. "I'll apply around town after my last final."

That was very unlike her sister. Elizabeth never waited till the last minute. That was Jessica's MO!

Elizabeth glanced at her watch. "Gotta go. I have to drop off my final, and then I'm meeting Nina. See you guys later." She scooped up her books and gave Sam a quick kiss, then hurried out of the kitchen.

"Good luck at the gallery," Neil said, standing up and collecting his notes. "Hope you get the job."

Yeah, me too, she thought, not totally sure if

she meant it. It sounded good. Really good. An art-history major working at a trendy gallery for the summer? Perfect, right? Wrong. Because despite how good it sounded on paper, Jessica wasn't so sure art was what she wanted to focus on. She really did love studying art history, but she wasn't positive she wanted to major in it after all. She wouldn't mind working at Yum-Yums, the fun campus café, for the summer. She wouldn't have to think beyond making coffee drinks and change. And that would give her time to figure out her entire life.

Well, her major, at least.

The phone rang, jarring her out of her thoughts. Sam was closest to it, but did he pick up the phone? Of course not. She got up and snatched it, shooting him his millionth dirty look. And it was only morning. "Hello?"

"Is Sam there?" asked a female voice. "This is his cousin Julia."

"Just a sec," Jessica said, handing the phone to Sam. She sat back down at the table. *Hey, wait a minute,* she thought, narrowing her eyes at him. Hadn't he given Elizabeth some sob story about how he had *no* contact with his family? So who was this cousin calling for him?

She nudged Neil's foot under the table, anxious to see what his take on the situation was. But Neil

6

was only paying attention to his political-science notes. *Whatever,* she thought, popping the last of her English muffin into her mouth. She had bigger things to worry about than Sam and his web of lies.

She'd mention this "cousin Julia" to Elizabeth later. Maybe that would finally wake up her sister and she'd dump the slacker!

"They only have size twos," Nina Harper complained as she rummaged through a stack of khaki pants marked fifty percent off. "Figures!"

"All the normal sizes are taken," Elizabeth said, following Nina to a rack of sundresses. "All the shopaholics hit the stores last month."

Elizabeth and Nina were hardly shopping freaks. They'd only agreed to this shopping quest in Sweet Valley's main-store district to outfit Nina for her summer job as a physics tutor for a high-school program.

Nina pulled out a floaty chiffon dress in a floral print. "Think this would work for a hot and stuffy classroom?"

Elizabeth laughed, then took the dress and held it against herself. "You know, I could use something like that." She checked herself out in the full-length mirror against the wall.

"You?" Nina said. "I'd never figure that for your style."

"You're right," Elizabeth agreed, "but I'm getting tired of oxford shirts and khakis."

"I hear you," Nina said. "I gave them up months ago. And now I need those kind of clothes for my job! Could you see me teaching some kid physics in thigh-high boots and a miniskirt?" She laughed. "Hey, what do you think of these?" She held up a pair of black cargo pants for Elizabeth's inspection.

"Perfect," Elizabeth said.

Nina folded the pants over her arm. "I guess I shouldn't be stressing so much about what to wear. This summer is about *learning*, not dressing hot to meet guys. I'm so psyched! I'll be teaching kids about string theory! Isn't that awesome? It's gonna be such a challenge. . . ."

"Yeah," Elizabeth said, nodding, trying to sound interested as she and Nina rifled through a rack of tank tops. She felt guilty that she wasn't really listening to Nina. But she was so involved in her own thoughts.

I used to be so much like Nina, Elizabeth thought as she followed her into the lingerie department. *So focused and driven. This has to be the first summer that I haven't lined up some amazing internship or fab job. Now that I've handed in my last final, the most pressing thing on my schedule is figuring out whether to go to the beach before lunch or to sleep late!*

"Hey, Elizabeth, what planet are you on?" Nina's voice interrupted her thoughts. "You look like you're pretty far away."

Elizabeth turned to face her friend. "Sorry, Nina, I was just zoning. Forgive me?"

"Of course." Nina eyed a lacy black bra with matching underwear. "Actually, I owe *you* an apology. I've been babbling on about myself, and I haven't even bothered to ask you what your plans are for the summer. So what are you doing? Let me guess—you've scored an internship with the *Sweet Valley News*!"

"Well, actually," Elizabeth began, "I haven't . . ." She trailed off as her attention was caught by a sexy black lace nightgown. *I wonder what Sam would think if he saw me in that.*

"Elizabeth! There you go again. C'mon, what's going on with you? I swear, you're totally spacing."

"Oh, Nina, I'm sorry I'm not very good company today. I've really got my mind on other things."

"No kidding!" Nina laughed. "I never noticed. You want to talk about it?" she asked sympathetically. "Did a job fall through or something? Is that why you haven't told me your plans?"

"Hardly." Elizabeth laughed. "In fact, I didn't even apply for any summer internships. To tell you the truth, my head's in the clouds because I can't

9

stop thinking about Sam. I'm really in love, Nina."

"In *love?*" Nina stopped rifling through a stack of cotton nighties and stared at Elizabeth. "You're sure? Really sure? We're talking actual *love,* not serious *like?*"

Elizabeth nodded happily.

"Wow." Nina seemed impressed. "You must be. Because if the ultra-ambitious and responsible Elizabeth Wakefield is changing her ways for a guy, then you know it's serious!" Nina squeezed Elizabeth's hand. "I'm really happy for you, Liz. I know what a roller-coaster ride it's been with Sam. You deserve to be happy."

"Thanks, Nina," Elizabeth said, her gaze wandering to the black nightie on display.

"Whoa!" Nina said, her dark eyes twinkling. "You are serious!"

Elizabeth grinned. "I don't know if I have the guts to buy it." She followed Nina into the dressing room and sat on the little stool by the mirrors. "You know what?" she asked.

"What?" Nina struggled out of her jeans and stepped into the cargo pants. "Tell the truth—are my hips really like that?" She looked at Elizabeth with a worried frown.

"It's definitely not your hips," Elizabeth assured her. Nina had a great figure. "It's the pockets—they're weird."

10

"Oh, well!" Nina said, unzipping the pants. "I'll find another pair."

"So, um, Nina," Elizabeth said. "I've got something really important to tell you. I think you'll be pretty surprised."

"What?" Nina pulled a baseball shirt over her head. "Though keep in mind that whatever you say, you couldn't shock me more than you already have. I mean, telling me that you haven't lined up a job, eyeing that sexy nightie . . ."

Elizabeth took a deep breath. "I think I want to sleep with Sam."

Nina looked at her in amazement for a few seconds. She finished pulling the shirt over her head, then sat down next to Elizabeth, looking her straight in the eye. "Okay, I take back what I just said—you *did* manage to shock me even more. Liz, are you sure about this?"

Elizabeth nodded. "Well, pretty sure. I feel like it's time to take the next step."

"But that's one heck of a step. I mean, it's giving up your *virginity*." Nina leaned back against the wall, her expression thoughtful. "Listen, Liz, I hate to ask this, but . . . do you think that you can trust Sam? I mean, he hasn't always been honest with you in the past."

Maybe I shouldn't have told Nina, Elizabeth thought, bristling in irritation. Why were people always bringing up his past mistakes? The fact was that Sam *had* lied to her—well, lied to Neil and Jessica too—and that didn't make Elizabeth very happy. But he'd explained himself to Elizabeth, and she'd accepted what he'd had to say. Shouldn't that be enough?

It wasn't even such a big deal, really. Sam had portrayed himself as a broke guy when he'd moved in with them. He was always eating the house-mates' food and borrowing a few bucks from everyone here and there. He had a beat-up car, wore jeans and black T-shirts, and didn't have much in terms of personal possessions, so Elizabeth had had no reason to think he was anything but what he seemed to be. But then she'd discovered that he came from a superrich family. That he'd disowned them and lived on a very small inheritance from his grandparents, just enough to cover his cheap tuition at OCC and pay his rent.

But it wasn't so much all that that had hurt Elizabeth so much. It was that he hadn't told her. Hadn't trusted her enough to share the truth, even as a friend. But more and more, Elizabeth had begun to understand why. Sam had serious problems with intimacy. That was why he'd always kept her at arm's length. That was why he'd avoided her after they'd finally kissed. That was why it had taken him so long to tell her how he felt about her. And tell her he was serious. That he wanted a real relationship.

That had only been last week. And so far, so good.

"Listen, Nina," she said firmly, turning to face her friend. "I *do* trust Sam totally. I trust him with my feelings. Okay, so he didn't come clean with his financial situation—he explained why he wanted to keep that a secret."

"Why?" Nina asked.

"Basically because he didn't want to talk about his family," Elizabeth explained. "It's really a sad situation, but from what he told me, they're not exactly the nicest people, Nina. He's totally estranged from them. His parents and his brother. And just because they're rich doesn't mean Sam's rich. He doesn't accept a dime from them."

Nina tilted her head. "Do you think he'll ever patch things up with them? I mean, not talking to your family has to be tough."

"I don't know," Elizabeth said. "I don't think so. Not for a while anyway. So, you see what I mean, right? About why I don't hold it against him. He didn't really lie at all. He simply didn't tell us about his parents. He's not pretending to be broke. He *is* broke."

Nina nodded. "And what about his little problem with commitment and intimacy, Liz? Do you think he's serious about committing to the relationship?"

"Yeah," Elizabeth said. "I do." And it was true. She did trust Sam. Not blindly. She wasn't stupid. But she was in love with the guy. And they'd been through so much this year. She desperately wanted their relationship to work. And she wasn't going to let skeptics like her sister or anyone tell her she was crazy.

Nina squeezed her arm. "I really am happy for you. I guess I'm just kind of stunned. I mean, deciding it's time to lose your virginity, being in love, not getting a summer job, going with the flow . . . sounds like a lot of changes. Are you bailing on the job thing because you want to spend more time with Sam?"

"Hey." Elizabeth laughed. "I said I was *thinking* about sleeping with Sam—I didn't say I'd already made up my mind. I don't know if I'm ready yet. And about working this summer . . ." She shrugged. "Listen, I'm supposed to be meeting my adviser in about twenty minutes, and I have a feeling I'm going to be hearing more than enough about that from him. In fact, I should get going."

Elizabeth stood up and reached for Nina's hand. "C'mon," she said, pulling her friend into a standing position. "Give me a hug."

"I'm going to miss you, Liz." Nina squeezed

her tightly. "And I hope you have a great summer, *whatever* you decide to do."

"I'll miss you too." Elizabeth picked up her backpack. She pushed open the dressing-room door. "Good luck with the rest of your shopping. Hey, don't forget to e-mail me, okay?"

"I miss you already." Nina smiled. "And if you do end up doing anything, I expect to hear about it! It'll sure make a break from string theory!"

"You nut." Elizabeth laughed as she closed the door behind her, but then tears sprang to her eyes. A whole summer without her best friend loomed ahead of her.

But so did a whole summer with the guy she loved!

Elizabeth felt stupid grinning her way down Sweet Valley Avenue, but she couldn't help herself. She rushed toward campus, not particularly looking forward to meeting with her adviser. She felt a brief twinge of nervousness as she imagined what their conversation would be like. Elizabeth hadn't been kidding when she'd told Nina that her adviser would be getting on her case about not having lined up an internship.

But that's not the half of it, she thought as she ran across the empty quad. Elizabeth had a feeling why she'd been called for a special meeting.

Because of the special programs she'd applied

15

to for the upcoming fall semester. Back when she'd been heartbroken over Sam and angry at her housemates, Elizabeth had applied for a few programs at different schools—just for the fall semester. She'd thought she needed a break from SVU, from her house, from her housemates—especially Sam. So she'd applied for two creative-writing programs as a visiting student, one in Boston and one in Chicago, and she'd been brave enough to apply for a semester-abroad program in London.

Elizabeth figured she'd been accepted to at least one of the programs, but then again, she couldn't be sure. She'd had to submit creative-writing samples, and being creative wasn't her strong suit. Journalism had always been her thing—facts. But in creative writing, you poured out your heart. And the truth and your heart didn't always agree.

So whether or not she did get accepted to one, she wasn't so sure she'd go. As she pulled open the door to Waggoner Hall, Elizabeth noted her reflection in the glass-pane door. She looked confused. If she'd been this much in love with Sam a few months ago, she would never have even bothered to apply. How could she possibly tear herself away from Sam for an entire semester? Their relationship was so new, so fragile.

Look on the bright side, Elizabeth thought as she

knocked on her adviser's door. *Maybe you weren't accepted to any of them.*

But she'd really wanted to get out of Sweet Valley at the time. And she'd knocked herself out on the applications.

Sam Burgess let out a frustrated sigh and headed out of bedroom into the living room. The phone call from Julia was really freaking him out. He had no idea what to do.

The minute he'd heard it was her, he'd told Julia he was running out the door to a final exam and would have to call her back. But he wasn't sure he wanted to call her back. Ever.

Julia was okay. In fact, he liked her. But he didn't need a twenty-minute lecture on how it was time to declare a truce with the Burgesses. Julia wasn't nuts about his parents either—hers were pretty much the same way. But she got along with her folks fine. And she thought Sam should forget their differences and have a perfectly nice, superficial relationship with them. That way, both sides could be happy. His parents could have their youngest son, and he could have parents.

But Sam wasn't interested. His parents weren't nice people, and they didn't deserve to have him in their life. They had Morgan, his older brother, and his two kids. That was enough.

Besides, they'd let Sam know what they thought of him two years ago, when he'd left for college.

"Hey, Neil," Sam said as he dropped down next to him on the hideous daisy-print sofa. "Can I unload on you for a sec?" He drummed his fingers nervously on his thighs.

"Yeah, sure, man," Neil said. "I guess I've studied about as much as I can." He stuffed his notes in his backpack. "What's up?"

"A lot." Sam exhaled raggedly, running a hand through his hair. "Before, um, in the kitchen? That was my cousin Julia on the phone." He smiled sarcastically at the look of surprise on Neil's face. "Yeah, yeah, I know. I told you guys that I never talk to my family. I'm sure Jessica thought Julia was some girl I met in a bar, *pretending* to be my cousin, but Julia really is my cousin. She's the only member of my family that I talk to."

Neil nodded, his gray eyes sympathetic. "So why'd you tell her you were heading out when you weren't? Why didn't you just talk to her?"

Sam leaned back his head. "I don't know—I guess I freaked a little. I just wasn't sure what she wanted. She likes to lecture me about the importance of family, and I can't take it sometimes." He paused and looked at Neil. "I just have a bad feeling about this one. Like she's gonna tell me my

18

dad's in the hospital getting a kidney stone removed and I have to rush home to Boston."

Neil chuckled. "Sam, look, you're not, like, some little kid here. You're a pretty big guy, and I haven't seen too many people mess with you. Well." Neil grinned. "Jessica *tries,* but really, I think you can probably handle this. If things get too sticky, you can always put on the brakes. Call her. For all you know, she's coming to town and just wants a place to crash."

"Maybe." Sam looked unconvinced.

"I gotta run." Neil stood up and stuffed his notes in his backpack. "My final's in half an hour, so I should get to campus."

"Yeah, good luck, and thanks, by the way."

"Call her," Neil said, sliding his backpack over his shoulder. He headed to the door. "She's family and the only one you like. So call her."

Sam nodded. He figured he'd wait till Neil closed the door. Then he figured he'd wait till the song he was playing on his stereo was over. Then he figured he'd wait till he made a sandwich.

In the kitchen Sam eyed the phone on the wall as if it were some kind of wild animal that could spring for his throat at any second.

"Oh, what the hell," he muttered, picking up the receiver and punching in the phone number that Julia had given him. He realized he was tapping his foot, waiting for her to pick up. *Jeez, Sam. Nervous much?*

"Sam!" Julia sounded really excited to hear from him. Sam could picture her pretty face, brown eyes, and short, pixielike auburn hair. "How'd your final go? That was fast, by the way."

Idiot, he told himself. *You should have waited another hour.* "Oh, yeah, um, it was an oral-presentation kind of thing. I think I did okay. So, what's up, Jules?"

"I'm getting married!" she screamed.

"That's great, Jules!" he said. "Congratulations!" Was that all? Sam felt immensely relieved. So Julia was getting married. Great, she'd found someone to love her. Someone she loved enough to spend the rest of her life with. Cool. Sam was psyched for her until he realized that getting married meant a wedding and a wedding probably meant that . . .

"Sam, I really want you to come to the wedding," Julia said. "It would mean the world to me."

Oh, man! This is so what I didn't want to hear!

"Look, before you say anything, I want you to think about this for a while," Julia pleaded. "I mean, it doesn't take a rocket scientist to know what your immediate reaction's going to be. But Sam?" She dropped her voice an octave. "C'mon, you know how close we used to be. How could you *not* come to my wedding?"

Sam closed his eyes, letting the waves of guilt wash over him. He remembered a family camping trip a bunch of years ago. Morgan, his older brother, had really done a number on him, telling ghost stories around the campfire. Sam had been terrified. His father had then sent him into the woods, alone, for ten minutes to see if he was "man" enough to deal with the fear. He'd been about to head off for his test; there was no way he'd admit how terrified he was. Even at eleven he'd been too much of a tough guy to show it. But Julia had seen through his mask, seen how frightened he was. She'd pretended that she was the spooked one and screamed until his dad had said he didn't have to do it. Then she'd insisted on sharing his tent.

It sounded dumb now, maybe, but such simple kindness had been rare in his family. She'd always been like that. Doing little things that told him how much she cared about him. And he'd returned the favor many times. But now she might be asking too much. "Julia," he began, "any chance that you're not inviting my parents?"

"Sam! You'd better be kidding. Look, I don't want to get in the middle of whatever's going on between you guys, but I know that your mother's really unhappy about the way things are. She'd be so psyched to see you. Seriously, she's broken-hearted over the rift. And I will be too if you're

21

not there to see me walk down the aisle."

Yeah, his mother was brokenhearted, Sam thought bitterly. That was why she'd sided with his father. That was why she called ever.

"Okay, okay." Sam groaned. "I get the picture. The only thing that's missing is the violins."

"Does that mean you'll come?" Julia sounded hopeful.

"It means I'll think about it," Sam promised.

"Thank you," Julia said quietly. "And Sam? I *know* you'll do the right thing."

"Yeah, the right thing would be to hop a freighter to Russia," Sam muttered to himself after they'd hung up. "I should never have listened to Neil." He shook his head. "That was my first mistake."

Sam wandered into the living room and collapsed on the couch. He reached listlessly for the remote, his mind reeling with the implications of Julia's bombshell. He knew that to anyone else, the situation would seem simple—his favorite cousin calling to invite him to her wedding. So what was the problem?

Plenty, Sam thought glumly. Because for Sam, family matters were anything *but* simple. He hadn't talked to his parents in almost two years, and he knew that if he went to the wedding, they'd be right in his face. *But what should I do? Am I going to let Julia down?*

Maybe I should talk to Liz, he considered. After all, no one was smarter or more caring than Elizabeth—if you needed a sympathetic ear, she was there. *Nah.* Sam shook his head. *She won't be able to get this one.* Elizabeth was totally into the family thing. She wouldn't be able to understand Sam's reluctance to see Julia, and she'd just put extra pressure on him to go to the wedding.

Okay, so talking to Elizabeth is out. Now what? Sam wondered, tossing the remote aside and staring at the blank screen. He'd planned a perfect day: a couple of hours on the couch, watching some classic cartoons, maybe hunting up Elizabeth on campus and having some lunch, then hooking up with his pals Bugsy and Floyd and shooting some pool. What could be better?

Only now things weren't so easy. Now he had to spend some major mental energy stressing about how he was going to tell his favorite cousin that he was going to break her heart.

Something he'd become way too good at.

Chapter Two

Okay, so what if you don't think you want to be an art historian, Jessica thought as she headed up the steps to the gallery. *It's a good summer job, you'll make money, meet some artsy guys.* Working at an art gallery would be totally cool. Scoring a real internship was the kind of thing Elizabeth always did; she totally focused and directed herself toward a *career.* Elizabeth wouldn't work behind the counter at Yum-Yums when she could work at a résumé-building job. So why should Jessica?

Besides, maybe she'd discover that she *did* want a career in art. Maybe by working at the gallery, she'd realize that she *did* want to continue on as an art-history major. The summer job would allow her to figure all this out. *Wow,* Jessica thought. *I sound like Elizabeth. Thinking, deciding—basing stuff on good reasons instead of what's easiest and most fun.*

24

Then again, Jessica figured, she was sure that a lot of fabulous, sophisticated, *wealthy* guys hung out there too. Or maybe even a few tortured, starving artists . . .

Hottie alert, closing in at fifty yards! Jessica's eye was caught by a truly gorgeous specimen sauntering down the steps. Brown hair with golden highlights (from the sun!), huge gray eyes, *perfect* build . . .

How should I start a convo? Jessica wondered. *He looks kind of familiar. Maybe I've seen him around the arts building? Maybe I should ask if he goes to SVU.*

"Hey, haven't I seen you around campus?" he asked.

Jessica flashed the guy a grin. He was even more handsome up close. She smoothed down the front of her blue linen dress, grateful that she'd taken extra time with her makeup before leaving the house.

"I'm Tyler Russell," he added, smiling at her.

Tyler was such a cool name.

"Jessica Wakefield." She paused, unsure of what to say next. *Oh, man, my flirting skills are way rusty,* Jessica thought ruefully. "So, gallery hopping now that you're all done with exams and everything, right?" *Duh! Like who isn't done with exams?*

25

"Yeah, I can't believe I'm finally going to be a senior," he said, revealing two perfect dimples. "It's almost scary. I mean, after next year it's the real world." He shifted several sketchbooks under his right arm.

"Do you draw?" Jessica asked.

"Yeah." Tyler smiled. "That's what's so cool about snagging the internship." He gestured toward the gallery. "I'm so relieved I got it. They said the competition was really tough, and there was only the one spot."

Jessica smiled. But before she could say anything, he continued. "They might even show some of my drawings as part of a student show. Wouldn't that be amazing? I don't know if I'm good enough for a show or anything, but it would be so cool!"

"So you've stolen my internship!" Jessica exclaimed in mock disappointment.

"Oh, hey, I'm really sorry," Tyler said, those incredible gray eyes full of concern. "I'm such an idiot! I was so psyched I got it that I didn't even realize you might be here to find out if *you* got it. Are you really upset? I mean, were you dying to work here this summer?"

Gorgeous and sensitive, Jessica thought. "Don't worry about it," she assured him. "I mean, I'm an art-history major, but I'm not all that sure that's the

26

way I want to go, you know? So, it's probably for the best that I didn't get it. It makes much more sense for you to work here if you really want to be an artist."

"That's really nice of you to be so generous about it." Tyler flashed her an incredible smile. "Painting is definitely the way I'm headed. I spent my sophomore year studying in Paris."

Could this guy be any more fab? Jessica asked herself. He was definitely the most exciting prospect she'd met in a long time.

"It must be nice to be so sure of what you want to do with your life," Jessica said almost wistfully. Even though she felt that she'd made some major changes in her life over the past year, she still worried that she'd never be as directed as someone like Elizabeth or, for that matter, Tyler. It sometimes seemed to her that everyone else had their whole lives figured out while she was just beginning to get a handle on hers.

"Sometimes it's cool," Tyler agreed. "But to tell you the truth, I kind of envy you."

"Me?" Jessica was dumbfounded.

"Yeah, because it's all ahead of you. You're not locked into any choices yet. Spontaneity. That's a pretty cool place to be."

"You're right," Jessica said slowly. She couldn't believe the way the conversation was turning out. Usually when she met a guy, he flirted by talking about superficial stuff, like the beach, his muscles, where he bought his watch. But Tyler seemed to have a certain sophistication to him. Jessica liked that. She couldn't wait to tell Lila about him—

"Omigod! Lila!" Jessica clapped a hand over her mouth.

"Should I ask?" Tyler raised an eyebrow.

"I'm so late for a lunch date!" Jessica exclaimed. She couldn't believe it. The best-looking guy, not to mention the most interesting, that she'd met in months, and she had to blow him off.

"Huh." Tyler nodded. Was it her imagination, or did he look slightly disappointed? "I take it Lila isn't a guy?"

"And if she was?" Jessica asked slowly, her heart thumping against her ribs.

"Well, if *she* was, then I wouldn't look forward to seeing you around town this summer," Tyler said with a sexy grin as he bounded down the rest of the steps. He stopped at the bottom and turned around to look at Jessica once more. "And I do look forward to seeing you around."

That makes two of us, Jessica thought. So, this summer might not be so bad after all. If she had to watch her sister and Sam sucking face in the backyard for three long months, she might as well have a hot summer romance of her own. . . .

*   *   *

"You don't seem very excited, Miss Wakefield," Professor Sedder said, peering at Elizabeth over his glasses. "You're the only student from SVU who was accepted to the University of London's semester-abroad program."

Elizabeth smiled weakly and squirmed in her seat. "It does sound wonderful." It really did. And if she weren't in love, she'd fly off in a heartbeat. Unable to meet the professor's gaze a moment longer, she stared at his collection of ballpoint pens.

"In fact, I'm almost glad that you didn't win the scholarships for the other two programs you applied to," Professor Sedder added. "The decision of which school to choose would be too much. This way you know exactly where you're headed this fall for one amazing semester! London!"

"I'm, uh, I'm honored," Elizabeth said. "I really am. I'm probably just shocked that I actually got accepted. A scholarship to a London college is a really big deal. . . ." She trailed off.

"It certainly is!" the professor said. "You should be very proud, Miss Wakefield. Very proud indeed."

You wouldn't be too proud if you knew I wasn't sure about going, Elizabeth thought. But how could she admit to the professor that Sam seemed more exciting, more challenging, and more wonderful than a semester abroad?

29

Am I choosing a "boyfriend" over an incredible opportunity? she wondered. *When it comes down to it, is that what I'm doing? And would that be so wrong?*

Somehow she felt embarrassed about admitting the truth, even to herself. *But how could I leave Sam?* she wondered. *We've just begun.* Elizabeth sighed, barely listening to Professor Sedder as he outlined the details of the program for her. She didn't need to listen. As far as she was concerned, she already knew the relevant details. If she accepted the scholarship, she'd spend the entire fall semester in another country. *The entire fall semester!* How could she possibly leave Sam for that long? A couple of weeks, maybe, but *months?*

"Thanks very much, Professor," Elizabeth said.

Professor Sedder smiled and handed her the letter. "Here you go. You can discuss your course of study with the adviser listed in the letter." He clapped. "This is so thrilling! I can see that you're stunned, Miss Wakefield. And with good reason!"

Good reason is right. Elizabeth almost smiled at the idea of telling ultraserious Professor Sedder that she was having boyfriend-on-the-brain issues. The man would fall off his chair! But perhaps he'd understand that her relationship with Sam was so new, so fragile, it could barely withstand the constant scrutiny of developing under Jessica and

Neil's noses. Could it possibly handle a separation of *continents*?

Elizabeth eyed the professor. No. He wouldn't understand. She had a feeling that no one would. This was the dream opportunity of a lifetime. You didn't turn it down.

But . . .

But who knows, she thought as she stood up to shake Professor Sedder's hand. Maybe the decision wouldn't be that hard after all. *Maybe something will happen that will make my decision completely clear.* Elizabeth had a brief vision of Sam following her to England . . . or maybe she and Sam would rent their own off-campus apartment, and Elizabeth would stay at SVU. Either seemed more appealing than spending the fall and winter in a foreign country where she knew absolutely no one.

Anyway, this was a decision she'd make herself. If she told Jessica, Jessica would probably drag her to London herself. Sam would probably tell her it was up to her. And her parents would freak.

Her head told her it was the opportunity of a lifetime. But her heart told her something quite different.

Sam walked along the main street in Sweet Valley, his hands deep in his pockets and a scowl on his face. He should never have called Julia back! He hated complications, and Julia's wedding was one big complication. If he let her down and didn't go, he'd feel terrible. And if he went and saw his family, he'd feel really terrible.

Boston. How the heck was he supposed to get there anyway? His car had a habit of breaking down on the way to OCC, which was only several miles away from his house. He couldn't afford a plane ticket, and there was no way he'd ask Julia to spring for his airfare. Some wedding present that would be!

So there it was. He couldn't go. He'd like to make Julia happy, but what could a guy do when he had no way of getting cross-country?

You could take a train or something, he thought, guilt washing over him. Argh! Truth was, he didn't want to go anywhere near Boston. He didn't want to be in the same room with his family. He couldn't. Wouldn't.

But this is about Julia. Not about you, jerk, he told himself.

What should he do?

Sam briefly considered going to SVU's campus to look for Elizabeth, but he pushed away the thought. He knew what he'd get from her. She'd be all bubbly and excited. She'd be thrilled at the idea of his reuniting with his family. Elizabeth, the most understanding girl he'd ever met, wouldn't understand his reluctance.

Give the girl some credit, he thought. *She's your girlfriend now. Of course she's the one you should talk to.*

Girlfriend. Now there was a label that would take some time getting used to. *My girlfriend.* Sam stopped dead in his tracks and then pivoted around. Find Elizabeth and get her take on the situation was exactly what he was going to do.

"Yo, Sam, over here!"

Sam whipped his head around and saw his buddy and fellow OCC schoolmate Bugsy waving at him from the opposite street corner.

"Hey, Bugs." Sam walked over to join him. "What's up, buddy?"

Bugsy grinned ruefully. "Finished my last exam yesterday—what a killer! I had one too many beers to celebrate, though. Talk about a hangover! So what's up with you, man?"

Sam pushed his baseball cap back on his head, wishing he could unload on Bugsy. The guy wasn't exactly known for his deep thoughts.

"Dude, check out the redhead closing in on the fifty-yard line." Bugsy elbowed him in the ribs. "Those are some knockers!"

Sam rolled his eyes. Usually Bugsy's girl radar made him laugh, but today he wasn't in the mood. "I've gotta hit the road, Bugs. I have to go find Elizabeth on SVU's campus."

"*Have* to find Elizabeth?" Bugsy repeated

incredulously. "I don't think so, dude. Has Wakefield affected your brain or what? This redhead's way hot! C'mon, guy, what's your move going to be?"

"You know I'm with Elizabeth now," Sam said wearily. And *he* knew Bugsy still refused to accept that as reality. As far as Bugsy was concerned, Elizabeth was nothing more than a priss. A beautiful priss, maybe, but a priss.

"With?" Bugsy asked, his brown eyes wide. "Try seriously tied down. Wakefield must have you on some tight leash if you're afraid to even *look*."

"I'm not afraid to look," Sam snapped. "I'm just not interested, okay? I have a *girlfriend*, Bugsy."

"Dude, you are so whipped!" Bugsy said.

"Whatever," he snapped at Bugsy. "Look, dude, you are way off."

Sam tried to act cool, but he was feeling anything but. *What's wrong with me?* he wondered. He *wasn't* tied down. He *wanted* to be with Elizabeth. There was a big difference. *Yeah, but Elizabeth can be pretty intense,* he thought. He hated how being "tied down" sounded. Why did Bugsy have to put it that way?

"I'm not afraid to look," he continued, swiveling his head to stare at the redhead. "But like I said, Bugs, I'm not interested."

34

—

"So I guess you're gonna ignore the fact that she's headed straight for us—and staring at you," Bugsy said under his breath. "Let's see the Burgomeister in action."

The majorly hot redhead, in tight, sexy jeans and a cropped pink T-shirt, smiled at Sam as she approached him and Bugsy. "Could you guys tell me how to get to the SVU campus?"

Her eyes were even bluer than Elizabeth's. *Stop it!* he told himself sternly. *You're not even supposed to notice something like that anymore.*

Or was he? So what that he noticed she had beautiful eyes? That didn't mean he wanted to know her name or ask for her number. He was just looking—not touching.

"Hey, Sam, aren't you headed to SVU *anyway?*" Bugsy asked, smiling innocently and looking from the redhead to him. "Why don't you just show this lovely young lady the way?"

Sam shot Bugsy a killer glare.

"I'd really appreciate it," the redhead said, her megawatt smile directed at Sam. "I'm a student at OCC, but I'm transferring to SVU this fall, so I wanted to have a look around."

"Uh, okay," he said slowly. "I am heading there, like my friend said."

"Great!" She looked at Sam like he was nothing less than a knight in shining armor.

"See ya, Sammy," Bugsy called as he headed down the street in the opposite direction. "Since you've got the afternoon free, you could probably show her around campus yourself."

"Would you?" she asked, looking hopefully at him. "I would really, really appreciate that."

"Well, um, I don't even go to SVU, so I don't think I could help," he said. "In fact, you know what?"

Was it Sam's imagination, or had she moved even closer to him? He suddenly found himself staring at her ample chest in that pink T-shirt. Man, the girl was built!

"What?" she asked, those blue eyes locked on his. She liked him. He could tell.

Suddenly Elizabeth's face came into his mind. His beautiful, sweet, intelligent Elizabeth. The girl he'd been through so much with this past year. No way was he going to mess that up for some hot redhead. Forget it!

"Look, um, I'm actually not going to SVU's campus," Sam said. "I was going to, but I just realized that I have to go do something."

She looked disappointed. "Well, I'll tell you what." She pulled a pen and a little piece of paper from her purse, then scrawled down her phone number. "Use this."

Sam smiled; he couldn't help it. He scored

even when he wasn't trying. Even when he was trying to be a good boyfriend. *You have some ego, Burgess*, he told himself.

All of a sudden, Sam felt eyes on him. Eyes other than the redhead's. He turned to the left, and the hairs on the back of his neck stood up.

Jessica! She was standing about ten yards away, giving Sam the evil eye. She locked eyes with him for a second, then turned and pranced off.

"Perfect." Sam groaned. Just what he needed. She'd clearly seen the girl give him her phone number. Her *unasked*-for phone number. Now Jessica would go running to Elizabeth and bust him. And for what? For turning down a busty redhead!

"See ya," the redhead chimed.

Sam glanced down at the number. Angela. Devila was more like it! Thanks to her, Sam was going to have to defend himself against what Jessica *thought* she saw. He could just imagine the night he was going to have.

"I can't believe that this time tomorrow, I'm going to be in France," Alexandra Rollins said dreamily, leaning back against the couch as Denise Waters expertly applied pale pink nail polish to her toes.

"I know—that totally rocks!" Jessica agreed as she flipped through a magazine and waited for her turn with Denise. The two Thetas, also two of Jessica's best friends, had come over to say good-bye before they took off for the summer. Denise was giving everyone farewell pedicures. "Hey, Denise, save some of that color for me, okay?"

"You got it," Denise said, blowing on Alex's pinkie toe.

Jessica put down the magazine on the coffee table, shot up, and began pacing the living room. "It seems like everyone else is going to have this amazing summer but me! Alex is going to France with her parents. Lila's going to be jetting all over as usual. What have you got lined up, Denise? Something equally fabulous, I'm sure."

"Pretty fab," Denise agreed as she finished Alex's toes. She gestured for Jessica to take her place on the couch. "I got an internship at a major PR firm in LA! They handle groups like the Red Hots and Phish."

"I am so jealous!" Jessica groaned as she flopped down on the couch.

Alex raised an eyebrow. "What happened to that art gallery you were so hot on?"

"Didn't pan out," Jessica replied as she kicked off her sandals to let Denise work her magic.

"That's too bad," Denise said sympathetically.

"Whatever." Jessica shrugged. "I mean, I don't think I'm going to end up in the art scene anyway, but it would have been a really cool place to work. I guess I'm just going to end up increasing my hours at Yum-Yums."

"Well, Yums is a fun place to work," Denise said. "They make the best lattes in Sweet Valley, if you ask me."

Jessica smiled. "Thanks, Denise."

"Hey, didn't Lila tell me that you ran into some amazing guy who'd scooped the job at the gallery?" Alex asked, wiggling her toes.

"Yup." Jessica wiggled her own toes, admiring the sparkly pink color. "That's true—he's way hot."

"So maybe the summer won't be a total wash," Denise said with a grin as she began packing up her supplies.

"Maybe," Jessica agreed absently. It was true that Tyler was a major hottie, but it wasn't like he'd even asked for her number or anything.

"Well, let me know what happens." Denise slung a flowered backpack over her shoulder and bent to give Jessica a hug. "I'll be checking my e-mail all the time."

"Yeah, me too." Alex blew her a kiss. "Have a great summer, Jess! You may be stuck on campus, but you've got Lizzie, right? And this Tyler guy sounds great. I'll bet you guys are, like, a major couple in a week."

Jessica laughed. "Here's to optimism! Hey, the next time I see you guys, we'll all be juniors!" She shook her head in amazement. "Have a great summer!"

The phone rang just as Denise was closing the door behind her. Jessica lunged for it as though it could possibly be Tyler. *Yeah, right, you fool. He probably wasn't interested!*

"'Lo?" she said, flopping onto the couch, careful not to smudge her beautiful new toes.

"Jessica? It's me, Carrie Lowell."

Jessica's heart stopped. "Hi, Carrie," she said, trying to sound nonchalant. Carrie was the current resident dean of Oakley Hall. Jessica had applied to be an RA, or resident adviser, during a fight with her housemates. She'd figured she'd never get the job. Jessica Wakefield was hardly known for her responsible side. With all the stress of exams, she'd forgotten she'd even applied. Plus she'd never move out of the house. She loved it here—even with Sam as a housemate!

"Jessica, congratulations!" Carrie exclaimed. "I'm calling to let you know that you'll be an Oakley RA for the upcoming fall and spring semesters!"

Jessica's mouth dropped open. "Yes!" She punched her fist in the air and did a small victory dance around the living room.

"That means you'll need to be up here for

freshman orientation," Carrie said, "instead of a week later with the rest of the upperclassmen. It also means you get your own single room."

Her own room? Hmmm.

No. How could she move out of the house? Neil had tried to pull something like that not too long ago, and Jessica had flipped out. So how could she turn the tables on him and move out herself?

"You're gonna be a great RA, Jess," Carrie said. "Congrats again!"

"Wait, I—" But Carrie had hung up.

Jessica clicked off the phone and stared at it. She'd been chosen to be an RA in the dorms. Her, Jessica Wakefield. It was almost unbelievable.

What had happened to the irresponsible fun seeker she'd been freshman year? *You replaced her, remember?* she reminded herself. With a girl who vowed to be more mature, take things more seriously. *And you did it.*

You really did it.

"Aaaahh! I can't believe it!" She jumped up on the couch. She couldn't remember feeling this happy in a long time. She wanted this post. Really wanted it. She'd gotten it, and now she wanted to prove she could handle it.

"Wow!" Jessica slid down until she was resting against the back of the couch. Being selected for

41

the RA position was like a total validation of all the changes she'd been trying to make for the past year. Last year the idea of anyone trusting her to give advice on anything but hair and makeup would have been a joke. But now she was going to be in a position of authority, dispensing wisdom to incoming freshmen, responsible for an entire floor of students!

The front door opened, and Jessica spun around.

"Hey, Jess," Neil said, kicking the door shut. He was carrying a bag from their favorite Mexican takeout. "I got you a burrito."

Omigod! Jessica looked at Neil, and her heart dropped about ten feet. *RA, Oakley Hall, moving out! What am I going to do without Neil? How am I going to be able to leave him and Elizabeth, not to mention our house?*

She looked around at the butter yellow walls with the burnt orange trim that she and Neil had painted together. That all seemed so long ago! Suddenly Jessica felt a lump in her throat.

"Thanks—I'm starving!" She smiled at him as he flopped down on the couch next to her. "Um, Neil? I've got, like, some *major* news."

He smirked. "Let me guess. Neiman Marcus is having a sale on leopard-print sundresses."

"Neil!" Jessica punched his arm. "You know

I'm not like that anymore. I mean, I don't *just* see college as a fashion opportunity. Besides, Lila told me that animal prints are totally passé." She reached for one of the tortilla chips that Neil was setting out. "No, really, I mean some *serious* news."

Neil regarded her thoughtfully over the top of his burrito. "So, are you going to keep me in suspense or what?"

"Actually, I am," she said. "At least for a couple of minutes. I think I should tell everyone at once." She got up and went to the bottom of the stairs. "Liz, Sam? Could you come down for a house meeting? Like right now?" She listened for footsteps from Elizabeth's attic room. "I don't think they heard me," she added to Neil.

"A house meeting?" Neil looked surprised. "Did Sam leave the butter out again, or did something really bad happen?"

"Nothing like that." Jessica shook her head as she walked up the stairs. "In fact, it's really good news, um, sort of. I mean, for me."

"Hey, maybe I should whip up some margaritas," Neil said, heading for the kitchen.

"Um, perfect!" Jessica smiled, but she couldn't help thinking that Neil wouldn't be around to whip up any margaritas at the drop of a hat once she moved into Oakley.

"What's going on?" Elizabeth asked, bending her head over the banister. Sam's darker head was behind her.

"House meeting," Jessica said. "Hey, don't look so sour, Sam. Neil's making margaritas."

"I'm there." Sam ambled down the stairs as Neil came back into the living room, holding a pitcher of frothy margaritas.

"So let's hear it." Elizabeth looked slightly worried. She squeezed Sam's hand tightly.

She probably thinks I'm going to squawk about something Sam did, Jessica thought, suppressing a grin. She stared at her twin for a second, realizing that when she moved into Oakley, they would be separated for the first time in nineteen years.

Twenty, she realized. In one month she and Elizabeth would celebrate their twentieth birthdays. They wouldn't be teenagers anymore.

Of course, Liz probably won't even notice, Jessica thought. *Her birthday or the fact that I'll be moving out in September. That's how stuck in Samville the girl is!*

"Okay, let's hear it," Sam said, settling against the couch in his habitual slouch.

Jessica took a deep breath. "Okay, you guys, you may think that you're looking at Jessica Wakefield, art-history major, soon to be junior and hippest housemate on the planet. But you're mistaken

44

'cause standing in front of you right now is the next Oakley Hall RA!"

"Whoa, Jess! That rocks!" Neil jumped up and threw his arms around her. "I mean, at least I think it does. Oh, man, I'm gonna miss you!"

"You're not mad?" she asked. "After the hard time I gave you when you thought about moving out?"

"Nah," he said, his gray eyes twinkling. "I'm not mad. I'll miss you to death, though."

"I know!" Jessica hugged him closer. "You can't imagine how much I'll miss *you!*"

"Hey," Elizabeth said. "I'm really proud of you, Jess. An RA! That's serious stuff! What am I gonna do around here without you?"

Jessica swallowed hard. "I can't imagine life without you either, Lizzie!" She reached out to include her in a group hug.

"You guys aren't gonna start bawling, are you?" Sam asked, smiling at Elizabeth.

Suddenly Jessica had a vision of Sam smiling at that slutty redhead who'd handed him what was obviously her telephone number. She'd deal with *that* later. Right now she wanted to only think about herself!

"You're going to miss Jess, right, Sam?" Elizabeth asked, stroking his hair.

Sam just stared at her. "Oh, yeah, big time."

Guess Sam's not too choked up at the thought of me leaving, Jessica thought, flashing him a cynical smile.

"Honestly, Jessica," Sam said, "I think it's great that you're going to be an RA. And I think that you owe me some serious thanks."

"Huh?" Jessica narrowed her eyes at him. "You wanna run that one by me again?"

"I mean it." Sam shoved a handful of chips in his mouth. "I totally trained you for this thing. It's going to be, like, so easy for you to rag freshmen about leaving soggy towels in the shower after dealing with me all year."

"You got that one right!" Jessica said as the room dissolved in laughter.

She stared at her sister, her best friend, and the jerk who made up her housemates, the crew she'd lived with since last September. She'd been through a lot with all of them. And she would miss them. Well, maybe not Sam.

Chapter Three

"Mmmm." Elizabeth stretched her arms over her head and smiled lazily. The feel of Sam's lips as they trailed butterfly kisses down her neck was utterly delicious. She snuggled closer, enveloping herself in his warm arms.

"I thought you'd never wake up," Sam murmured, tightening his hold around her.

"Why? What time is it?" Elizabeth turned over and squinted at the alarm clock. "It's only nine-thirty!"

"I know, but you're usually up at, like, six," he said, kissing her hair. "I have to say, it's nice getting up earlier than you for once. I get to watch how cute you look when you sleep." Sam gave her a lopsided grin and twirled a strand of her hair around his finger.

"Hey, cut me some slack! Nine-thirty isn't

exactly late, and I *did* just finish all of my exams." Elizabeth grinned. It felt great that the semester was finally over. It felt even better to have sailed through her exams with straight A's. *But nothing, nothing, feels better than waking up in Sam's arms,* Elizabeth thought as she looked into his gorgeous face. She could stare into his hazel eyes and gaze at his silky sandy-brown-blondish hair forever.

She still couldn't get over the fact that they were sleeping together—well, they weren't *sleeping* together, but she and Sam spent most nights in either her bedroom or his. They were in his room now. Last night, like all nights they spent together, they kissed and kissed and kissed. Just lying in his arms all night felt incredibly intimate—and incredibly good.

It feels better than anything I could have imagined, Elizabeth thought dreamily as she stared at a patch of yellow sunlight on the floor. It felt so good that she couldn't help wondering what it would feel like to take the next step. Elizabeth shivered slightly as she imagined the possibility. It would feel scary. She knew some girls who said that it hurt the first time. She imagined Sam on top of her, moving even closer. . . . It would feel strange at first. It would feel . . .

It would feel wonderful!

Elizabeth turned over on her stomach and propped her elbows on Sam's chest. Her blond hair tumbled around them like a curtain as she looked down at him with a small smile on her face.

"You look all mysterious all of a sudden." Sam raised an eyebrow. "What are you thinking about?"

That I want to make love to you.

The thought slammed into Elizabeth's head, and she blinked in surprise. Had she, Elizabeth Wakefield, virgin, nineteen, journalism major, soon to be junior, really just thought that? Where had *that* come from?

It's been building for a while now. She thought back to her conversation with Nina a few days ago. She'd been considering it then, but now she was doing more than just considering. Elizabeth brushed a kiss against Sam's cheek and wrinkled her nose at how scratchy his stubble was.

"So, c'mon," Sam prodded. "What's running through that incredibly complicated mind of yours?"

"I was just thinking that you need to shave." Elizabeth cocked her head. Should she really tell him what was going through her mind?

"Right now?" he asked.

Elizabeth didn't answer; her mind was too filled with images of them having sex, and it was making it difficult for her to speak. She could hardly believe she was thinking these things. Visualizing these things.

Did she really feel ready?

Yes.

The realization almost took her breath away. Maybe she was rushing things. Maybe it was too big a step for them to take. Elizabeth leaned back a little and looked deep into Sam's hazel eyes. His tousled hair and sexy grin made him look just like a little boy. But Elizabeth knew that he wasn't a little boy. Far from it.

Although Sam was difficult at times, he'd often displayed a maturity and tenderness that she found incredibly moving. Sure, he had problems, as Jessica never tired of pointing out, but he was also smart, sensitive, loving, and sexy. Elizabeth stroked his unruly hair as she thought of how much they'd been through together.

Things hadn't been storybook perfect between them. They'd gotten off to an incredibly rocky start, and even now there were still plenty of speed bumps, but that didn't change the fact that Elizabeth felt closer to Sam than she ever had with any other boyfriend. And it didn't change the fact that her whole body felt charged with electricity just from lying on top of him. She could feel the heat from his bare chest through the skimpy fabric of her T-shirt. Skin-to-skin contact with the guy she loved. What would that feel like?

She wanted to lose her virginity with Sam.

Wow. So this is what it feels like to be ready. This is what it feels like to really want to make love to someone.

"Sam," Elizabeth murmured.

"Hmmm?" Sam stroked her hair lazily. He seemed to be falling back asleep.

"Sam." Elizabeth moved her head to whisper in his ear. "I'm ready, Sam." Just saying the words was exciting. She *was* ready. In fact, now that the time had come, she could hardly wait.

"Ready for what?" Sam asked, his eyelids fluttering closed. "Ready to go downstairs and make breakfast?"

"No. To make love with you," Elizabeth said simply.

"That's weird," Sam murmured. "I thought I was awake, but I guess I'm still asleep and having this amazing dream." He moved to turn on his side and buried his head deep in one of the pillows.

Elizabeth blinked in surprise. This was *not* the reaction she'd expected—to say the least. "Sam," she said a little more insistently. "You're not having a dream." She shook his shoulder very gently.

"I'm not?" Sam half opened one of his eyes and looked at her in confusion. "Are you sure?"

Elizabeth nodded firmly.

Sam's eyes opened all the way. "Did you just say that you were ready to have sex?" He sat bolt

51

upright and stared at Elizabeth. "Are you sure you know what you're saying, Elizabeth?" He reached for her hand and squeezed it tightly. "I mean, we're talking about a pretty big deal here."

Elizabeth smiled at the expression on his face. He seemed incredibly touched, maybe a little scared too, but definitely very moved.

"Yeah, I know," she said. "Believe me, I know. But it just seems like the next step. It just feels *right* between us, Sam."

"Liz, I'm really, really, like, I don't know what to say—*honored* that you feel like you can sleep with me." Sam ran a hand through his hair "I mean, I'd love to. . . ." He trailed off uncertainly.

"Why do I feel like there's a *but* at the end of that sentence?" Elizabeth said.

"Well, 'cause there is." Sam increased the pressure on her hand. "Of course I *want* to sleep with you, Elizabeth. Man, I'd be crazy not to want to, but I just think that maybe you're rushing things."

"That's supposed to be my line!" Elizabeth protested.

"Okay, well, this time it's mine. Look, I'm just saying that I don't want to rush you. I know what a hard time you had with that jerk Finn."

Elizabeth didn't want to be reminded of Finn Robinson, who she'd almost lost her virginity to. *Almost* being the key word. She'd known she wasn't ready. Even though she'd tried to force herself to believe she was. At the moment of truth, she'd been unable to go through with it. But she knew that she was ready now. Knew it in her heart.

"Sam," she began, but he cut her off.

"Look, Liz," he said, his eyes full of tenderness. "I know what a big step this is, and I want you to be totally ready. We can take our time. We've got all summer to get closer to each other. I don't want you to regret anything." Sam paused; he seemed to be struggling to find the right words. "I just want it to be incredibly special for you," he said quietly. "Something beautiful."

Elizabeth stared at Sam in shock. *So much for the insensitive cad that Jessica's always warning me about,* she thought. It wasn't that she was surprised that he could be so thoughtful; it was just that, well, it seemed kind of amazing that he wasn't jumping at the offer. Elizabeth had practically broken up with her last three boyfriends because she wouldn't have sex with them, and now here was Sam telling her to take her time. Telling her that he wanted things to be beautiful. She couldn't help feeling a bit disappointed, but more than anything else, his reaction told her that she'd made the right decision.

"Thank you for being so incredibly thoughtful,"

Elizabeth said softly. She brushed a kiss against Sam's shoulder.

"Personally, I think I'm being really stupid, and I'll probably kick myself later," Sam muttered, flinging back the covers and jumping out of bed. "I think I'm gonna hit the shower." He began whistling a tune off-key. "You seen my Bugs Bunny T-shirt?" he called over his shoulder.

"I think I see it sticking out from under the bed, next to those candy wrappers." Elizabeth shook her head, amazed that she'd ever managed to fall in love with someone as sloppy as Sam. She got out of the bed and walked over to the wrappers. "Uh, Sam? I think you might want to give it a wash or three before you wear it, though." Even from where she was standing, Elizabeth could see the tomato-sauce stains on it.

"You think?" Sam bent to pick it up.

"Yeah, I think," Elizabeth said firmly. She pulled the chair out from behind Sam's desk and sat down as she watched him root around for another shirt. "Hey, what's this?" The corner of a fancy envelope caught her eye. It was sandwiched between a couple of CDs and a burrito wrapper. She fished it out with two fingers, surprised by the thick, creamy paper and the embossed writing.

"Huh?" Sam was busy sniffing the armpits of a Road Runner sweatshirt. "Oh, that. That's just an invitation to my cousin Julia's wedding. She's, like, the only person in my family I still talk to."

"She's getting married?" Elizabeth opened the envelope and scanned the card.

"Yeah, that's what a wedding invitation usually means."

"Sam, that's so fantastic! You have to go!" Elizabeth knew that she was treading on dangerous ground. Sam had been estranged from his family for close to two years. And it wasn't something he liked to get into with her. As close as she was with her own family, Elizabeth couldn't imagine how much she would suffer if she were cut off from them. Of course, Sam always insisted that he couldn't stand his family, but she knew that deep down, he had to have a lot of pain about the situation. She was sure that going to his cousin's wedding would be a great way to heal the past.

"And deal with my mother and father?" Sam's sarcastic voice cut into her train of thought. "Uh-uh, no way. We could pose for, like, some public-service announcement for dysfunctional families."

"But Sam, you should . . ."

Sam wheeled around to face Elizabeth, the tenderness in his face was completely gone. "Believe me, Elizabeth, I've thought about this pretty carefully. I was going to talk to you about it a few days ago, but then I decided I needed to figure it out for myself. And I have. I've been pretty tight with Julia in the past, and I feel crappy about letting her down, but I just can't handle the emotional price tag that would come with going to the wedding."

"Sam, I—"

"Listen, Liz, you want to talk about what to have for breakfast? Great. You want to talk about what we should do this summer? I'm there. You want to talk about my family? Sorry. Discussion closed. Now, I'm going to take a shower. Why don't you figure out what you want to do for breakfast while I'm doing that? Should we steal some of Jessica's Cap'n Crunch, or do you want to go out?"

"How 'bout we go out," Elizabeth said quietly as he marched off to the bathroom.

You may think you're not going to talk about your family, Elizabeth thought as she heard the shower start. *And you may think that we're not ready to have sex yet. But Sam Burgess, you're in for a couple of big surprises this summer!*

Jessica reached up toward the top shelf and grabbed a bag of coffee filters. Unfortunately they weren't balanced very well, and the entire stack toppled down onto her head. "This is definitely *not* going to be my most happening summer,"

Jessica muttered as she stacked the fallen bags back on the shelf. Grabbing one of the vanilla hazelnuts, she dumped it into the grinder.

She was in the back room at Yum-Yums, making sure that they had enough freshly ground java for all the hordes of people that were outside clamoring for their double-mocha lattes and their lemon bundt cakes. Ordinarily she didn't mind working at Yums; the pay was good, and the free samples were cool. But while it had been a great way to earn a little extra cash during the semester, it *wasn't* the way Jessica had pictured spending her summer. Still, now that the job at the gallery was taken, she didn't have anything else on the horizon. In fact—Jessica sighed—she was probably going to expand her hours into full-time.

"Great, so Lila will be jetting all over the place. Alex will be in France, lounging in castles or whatever, Denise is going to be hanging out with the Red Hots, and *I'm* going to be asking people if they want skim or half-and-half." *And now I'm talking to myself!* she thought, rolling her eyes.

Still pouting, she pushed open the door with her hip and carried the coffeepot into the main room. Her face fell as she saw who was waiting first in line to be served. *Sam and Elizabeth.*

Like it's not bad enough that I have to watch my sister drooling all over that slacker at home, she thought bitterly. *Now I've got to serve them too?*

"Hey, Jess," Sam said. "How about two iced capps and a couple of brownies? Breakfast of champions."

"Coming right up," Jessica said, rolling her eyes again. She was grateful to turn her back on Sam, the biggest liar in Sweet Valley, while she made their drinks. She hadn't mentioned catching him flirting with the redhead to Elizabeth; Jessica was tired of listing Sam's many crimes and being told to mind her own business. Besides, because of her own excitement over the RA post, she'd forgotten about seeing that girl hand Sam her phone number. Worse, Elizabeth looked so darn happy lately that Jessica couldn't bear to mention it. After all, just because Jessica saw the redhead give Sam her number didn't mean he'd called the girl. Did it?

"Here." Jessica plunked a tray with their drinks and the brownies on the counter between them. "That's nine bucks," she added to Elizabeth, knowing that Sam never paid for anything. Her jaw dropped as she watched Sam take a pile of bills out of his pocket and peel a couple off the top. *He must have lifted a twenty from Neil's wallet,* Jessica thought snidely.

"I'm going to get us a booth," Sam said, picking up the tray.

58

"I'll be with you in a sec," Elizabeth said, smiling at him. "I just want to talk to Jess for a second."

"What's up?" Jessica busied herself with wiping down the counter.

"Why are you so down on Sam?" Elizabeth asked peevishly. "Never mind." She held up her hand as if warding off Jessica's reply. "I know all about why you don't like him. But do you think you could at least act civil?"

Jessica looked at her sister. *Should* she tell her about that little scene she'd witnessed between Sam and the redhead the other day? Probably not, she decided again. It wasn't enough of a big deal to risk getting Elizabeth pissed at her. She knew that's what would happen too: Elizabeth would be mad at *her* for telling her, not mad at *Sam* for flirting.

"Whatever." Jessica shrugged. She knew that nothing she did would change Elizabeth's mind. Her sister would just have to find out about Sam the hard way. Still, Jessica was amazed that somebody as incredibly smart as Elizabeth could be so stupid about some things. "Okay, I'll cut the guy some slack. Just stop giving me that look." She gestured toward the booth where Sam was slurping his capp. "Shoo. I've got to work."

"Could I get a . . . Jessica!"

Jessica peered behind Elizabeth to see Tyler

smiling at her. "Tyler! What are you doing here?" She blushed. "Stupid question. You want a cup of something!"

"Actually, I was walking by and I saw you through the window," he explained, his dimples popping out as he smiled shyly. "I thought I'd ask how the internship search is going."

Hmmm. Is he interested, or is he just a nice guy? "I've given up," Jessica admitted, shrugging. "Not to make you feel guilty, but you bagged the only good job in town." He laughed, and she smiled, biting her lip. "But seriously, it's kind of late to look for something, and Yum-Yums isn't that bad. I've been here part-time for a while now, and I think I'll go full-time if they'll let me." She paused, sure that she sounded like a dumb kid. What would a sophisticated painter like Tyler think of her plans? "That probably sounds really lame to a serious artist like you."

"Are you kidding?" Tyler looked at her in amazement. "It sounds really disciplined of you. If I hadn't gotten an internship that I'd been into, I'd probably have spent the rest of the summer sulking, not increasing my hours. And this seems like a really cool place to work, Jessica."

Jessica beamed. Discipline and Jessica Wakefield didn't usually come together in the same sentence.

"But even though I can see that you're incredibly hardworking," he began, his gray eyes staring into hers, "they must let you catch a break sometime, right?"

"Right." Jessica gave a slow smile.

"In fact"—Tyler leaned closer—"you look like you could use one now. Can I buy you an iced mochaccino and one of those really decadent looking pastries?"

"I think I could handle that," Jessica said, turning to make their drinks. "But you don't have to buy—it's on the house."

"Huh." Tyler nodded thoughtfully. "In that case, I'll have to pick up the check some other time." He pointed at two chocolate-caramel brownies in the display. "Those look great."

Jessica poured their drinks into glasses, set them on a tray, and added the brownies. "Hey, Cathy," she called to the back room. "Can you cover for me?"

A cute brunette rushed out of the back door. She tied her apron, winking at Jessica. "You bet. Oh, and just in time for the crowd!"

Jessica laughed as she eyed the group pushing their way through the double doors into the café. She scanned the large room for Tyler; he was sitting at a table near the faux fireplace.

Now, what did he mean by picking up the check

some other time? Jessica wondered as she joined him. Was he going to ask her out?

Her gaze ran over his supercute face, his long, lean body, his mysterious gray eyes. *Please, please, please!* she thought.

Suddenly the summer didn't seem quite so bleak.

"It feels so weird to be here," Elizabeth said, gesturing toward the quad. "I mean, I don't think I've ever seen the campus this empty. It's like a ghost town or something."

She and Sam were holding hands as they walked slowly across the lawn. Ordinarily they would have had to step over hundreds of sunbathing students, but today the only thing in their path was a small squirrel that scampered away as they approached.

"Yeah, well, finals are over—people don't want to hang around campus anymore," Sam said. He sounded preoccupied.

Elizabeth stole a glance at his profile. *What's going on in that incredibly complicated head of his?* she wondered. He'd been unusually silent all morning. *Ever since he told me about the wedding,* she realized with a start.

Elizabeth was convinced that Sam should attend. The only problem was, how was she going to convince him of the same thing? As far as she was concerned, going to the wedding would be the perfect way to patch things up with his family. She'd tried to explain that to him over breakfast at Yum-Yums, but he'd just shrugged and abruptly changed the subject. Still, Elizabeth wasn't about to be put off that easily, especially about something this important.

"You want to sit on the grass for a while?" Sam interrupted her thoughts.

"Sure," Elizabeth said. They wandered over to a magnolia tree and sat down underneath its fragrant blossoms. Sam stretched his long legs out in front of him and leaned back against the trunk, then pulled his baseball cap down low and closed his eyes.

Elizabeth gazed at his profile intently for a long moment, unsure whether it was a good time to return to the subject.

Sure, it is, she tried to convince herself. *He's so relaxed, it's the perfect time. He was just really stressed at Yums. Plus the fact that Jess was there didn't make things any easier.*

"Sam?" she began tentatively.

He opened one eye and looked at her.

Elizabeth paused and took a deep breath. "I know you'd rather have a root canal than talk about the wedding, but I really think it's important."

"How about a root canal without novocaine?" Sam asked irritably. "Listen, Elizabeth, I know that you mean well; you just want everybody to be one big, happy family the way yours is, but sorry, it doesn't work that way."

"But Sam." Elizabeth sat up on her knees and looked at him with pleading eyes.

"But nothing," Sam said harshly. "Hey, I'm really sorry." He reached for her hand and gave it a squeeze. "I guess I should be touched that you care so much, but trust me, this is a closed subject, and besides, it has nothing to do with us."

"That's not completely true, Sam," Elizabeth said quietly. She averted her eyes and began searching through the grass for a four-leaf clover.

"Yeah? Just how does this involve us?"

How can I tell Sam that I'm worried about what this could mean for the two of us? Elizabeth was silent for a minute. *How can I tell him that it scares me that he can walk away from his family so easily? If he can leave them like that, could he just walk away from me too? And that he'd even let down the one family member he likes tells me a lot. Too much, maybe.*

"I think I got it," Sam said, sounding bitter. "You think the fact that I can't deal with my family means that I can't handle commitment, period."

Elizabeth's head snapped up, and she looked at

Sam in amazement. She knew that when Sam wasn't kidding around, he could be incredibly insightful. It was one of the things she loved most about him, but still, she couldn't help feeling surprised. It was almost as if he had read her mind. "Well, *does* it mean that?" she asked softly.

"No," Sam said emphatically. "I don't hang with my family for a lot of really complicated reasons. I've told you about it, Liz. It's them. It's not because I'm weird or can't deal. They're nasty, cold, unfeeling people who only care about money and appearances. Look, you can't choose your relatives, but you *can* choose your . . . your . . . significant other," he added, stumbling over the words.

Significant other? Elizabeth looked up quickly. He'd never called her that before. Did it mean anything? Was it a measure of how serious his feelings really were for her? No matter what he said, Elizabeth knew that he really was afraid of commitment, but maybe deep down he was trying to work on things. *Maybe I should cut him some slack,* she thought, noticing that Sam was looking pretty uncomfortable.

He can't handle the way I'm pressuring him. I'll forget about the whole family thing for a while; I'll stop stressing about us and just enjoy our time together. . . .

"So, how about we hang out at the beach?"

65

Elizabeth forced herself to sound cheery. "Just relax and veg out."

"Uh, actually I kind of promised Bugsy and Floyd that I'd help them pack up their dorm room." Sam didn't look at her as he spoke. "I should probably be heading over to the OCC campus now."

Elizabeth's heart sank. She had a strange feeling that he would have been perfectly happy to blow off Bugsy and Floyd if she hadn't brought up commitment issues.

But what can I do now? If I call him on it, he'll only get defensive. "Um, okay, sure," she said, trying to appear unconcerned. "I'll see you later." She leaned back against the tree and took a book out of her backpack. "I'm just going to hang here and read for a while."

Sam nodded. "Okay, see ya." He walked off without looking back.

Damn! Elizabeth slammed down her book in frustration. *That is not how I wanted things to go! I better chill on this whole wedding thing,* she thought. Because one thing was for sure, she realized. The quickest way to get close to Sam was to be ultra-low-key, and the surest way to push him away was to push him too far.

And close was what she wanted to be.

Chapter Four

Sam squinted and threw the dart with perfect concentration. It landed smack in the center of the bull's-eye, and he turned to Floyd with a triumphant smile on his face. He'd been hanging with Bugsy and Floyd for the past couple of hours. After helping his friends pack up their dorm room, he'd decided to head with them over to Frankie's bar and play a couple of rounds of darts.

"Let's see you top that, dude," Sam challenged as he sauntered back to the table and took a long pull on his beer.

"Yo, you were, like, standing way close," Floyd complained.

"Yeah, like I can't hit a bull's-eye from halfway across the room anyway." Sam collapsed into a chair and reached for the basket of potato chips in the center of the table. "You're just jealous."

"Jealous," Floyd hooted. "Right. Listen, dude, I'm totally cool. I—"

"Oh, like who cares," Bugsy interrupted impatiently. "We all know that Sam's a great dart player. I don't want to hear you guys yakking about that. I want the scoop!"

"What scoop?" Floyd turned to him, surprise on his doofy face.

"Well," Bugsy said, walking to the table and drawing a chair up close to Sam. "I'm actually interested in hearing about how good Elizabeth Wakefield is in bed."

"Yeah, I could get into hearing that," Floyd added enthusiastically.

"Guys." Sam sat up and glared at them. "You're talking about my girlfriend. So how about shutting up?"

Bugsy grinned. "C'mon, man! Spill it! Is she good? Prissy?"

Sam aimed a dirty look at Bugsy, ignoring his question.

"I know why you're getting so uptight all of a sudden," Bugsy said, eyeing Floyd. "Hey, Floyd, what are you betting old Sam doesn't want to tell us how she is in bed because he doesn't *know?*"

Sam buried his head in his arm. He didn't know how to respond to Bugsy, and he didn't know how someone could change from being such a great guy to hang out with to a total jerk in a matter of seconds.

"Get out of here!" Floyd's jaw dropped. "C'mon, Sam, set the guy straight. You're sleeping with Elizabeth, right? I mean, dude, you've been going out for, like, *weeks*."

"Get real, Floyd," Bugsy said. "Are you forgetting what a total priss she is? Forget having sex—they probably haven't gotten *naked* together."

"Sam." Floyd looked at him in alarm. He walked over to the table and sat down next to Bugsy. "What are you doing with someone like that? She's not for you, man."

"For your information," Sam said through gritted teeth, "*I'm* the one putting on the brakes in the sex department." He felt so uncomfortable talking with them about the intimate details of his and Elizabeth's relationship, but he didn't know how else to shut them up.

"Give me a break," Bugsy said. "Like you're not dying to sleep with her!"

Sam could see why Bugsy would have a hard time believing that one. After all, what guy in his right mind wouldn't want to sleep with Elizabeth Wakefield?

He thought back to earlier that morning, when she'd told him that she was ready to make love. Most guys would have been thrilled to have a girlfriend like Elizabeth offering themselves sexually, but her revelation had had a totally different effect on Sam. It had spooked him royally.

Could he really take away sweet, innocent Elizabeth's virginity? Was *he* ready for that? Sure, Sam had been around before, but all the girls that he'd been with knew the score. Elizabeth was different. What if he hurt her physically? He was sure that however their lovemaking turned out, he'd hurt her *emotionally*. Because Elizabeth had stars in her eyes. Sam could just tell.

Yes, he really cared about her, maybe even more than that, maybe even a *lot* more than that, but that was where he was at today. He didn't know where he'd be five years from now or even five minutes from now.

But Elizabeth wasn't like that. She had her whole life mapped out, and right now she saw Sam as a key player. Oh, sure, she'd never mentioned things like moving in together or *marriage*—Sam shuddered involuntarily—but she wouldn't have felt ready to sleep with him if she didn't feel comfortable with having Sam in the picture for a long, *long* time.

He gave Bugsy a cynical smile. "Hey, think what you want, dude, but I'm not into sleeping with her before we're together for a while. She's not just some girl I'm trying to score with, okay?"

"Explain yourself, man," Floyd said.

Sam toyed with his beer glass. He had to keep his hands occupied; otherwise they would wrap themselves around Floyd's throat. "She's a virgin," he finally said, grabbing a potato chip. "You know how that works—you sleep with a virgin, they get all clingy. I don't hang with that stuff." Even as he said the words, he felt like he was betraying Elizabeth. He wasn't quite sure how much was true and how much he'd said for his friends. At least the explanation would shut them up.

"Now you're talking sense." Bugsy nodded. "I mean, virginity, that's, like, tough to deal with. And Elizabeth, she's so straight, she must be, like, a virgin squared or something."

"Cubed, dude!" Floyd declared. "Yeah, I got the picture now," he added in a bored voice. He picked up a handful of darts and moved away from the table.

At least I got them off my back, Sam thought in relief.

So why do I feel so awful all of a sudden? Is it their probing questions or the fact that I'm bizarrely turning down my girlfriend for sex? I can tell her it's her who's not ready all I want. And she'll probably believe me. But it's me who's not ready.

71

Not ready to deal with the consequences of being the guy who took Elizabeth Wakefield's virginity.

"That smells fab, Neil!" Jessica said as she pushed her way into the kitchen through the swinging door. "What are you making?" She sniffed the air appreciatively as she unwrapped the towel tied turban style around her head and started drying her hair vigorously.

There was nothing better than waking up late, taking a long, hot shower, and entering the kitchen to find your best friend cooking something yummy. Elizabeth and Sam were nowhere to be seen, which was more than fine with Jessica because she was looking forward to a long gossip with Neil *without* any untimely interruptions from Sam.

"Just whipping up a batch of my ultradelish banana-walnut pancakes," Neil said, grabbing a spatula and flipping one over.

"Any for me?" Jessica asked.

"If you're extra nice." Neil grinned and slid a couple of pancakes onto a plate. He handed it to Jessica.

"Totally amazing," Jessica said, grabbing the bottle of maple syrup from the refrigerator. She sat at the table and doused her pancakes in syrup. "But you know what's even more amazing? The fact that I met this awesome guy, and I haven't even had a chance to talk to you about it."

"So talk," Neil said, sitting down next to her. "C'mon, I'm more than interested in hearing about awesome guys."

Jessica laughed. "Sorry, Neil, this one's straight. At least, I hope so. I mean, he hasn't asked me out or anything yet."

"Matter of time," Neil said. "So c'mon, get to the good stuff. What does he look like?"

"Completely and totally gorgeous." Jessica smiled. "Golden brown hair, gray eyes, lanky but muscular build . . . actually, he kind of looks like you!"

"Hey, who can beat that?" Neil asked modestly.

"Who can?" Jessica took a sip of coffee. Neil *was* gorgeous. She'd been heartbroken when Neil had told her that he was gay, but after the initial shock had worn off, she'd learned to deal with it pretty well. If she couldn't have Neil as a boyfriend, she'd be very happy to keep him forever as her best bud.

"What's he do, where'd you meet him, when are you seeing him again—c'mon, Jess, *info*."

Jessica grinned. "Okay." She put down her cup and shifted in her chair to get more comfortable, hugging her knees to her chest. "Well, to add to his near perfection, he wants to be a painter!"

"Artsy," Neil interrupted. "Very good, Jess."

"I know." Jessica nodded happily. "The only problem is, I don't know when I'll be seeing him again. I mean, he came into Yums because he saw me through the window, or so he said, but we hung out for a while on my break, and he didn't ask me out!"

"Five bucks says he will."

Jessica looked at Neil hopefully. "Well, I don't know about that, but I do know that the summer might not be so bad after all." She took a bite of her pancakes. "I've got something possible maybe happening with Tyler; Yum-Yums isn't such a lousy place to work." She shrugged. "So what about you? When are you leaving for camp?"

"Couple of days." Neil toyed with his pancakes. "I'm gonna miss you. And when I get back, you'll be moved into Oakley."

"That's only a mile away," she pointed out. "We'll be back and forth visiting each other all the time. Hey, so, psyched about the counselor job?"

"Totally," Neil said, sipping his coffee. "It's like a paid summer vacation. I mean, I'll get to swim, work on a tan—"

"Deal with a bunch of screaming twelve-year-olds all day," Jessica said, laughing.

"Don't I know it," Neil agreed. "But I love kids—"

He was interrupted by the trill of the phone ringing. Neil jumped up and grabbed it. "Hello? Uh, yeah, just a sec." He turned to Jessica with a grin. "It's Tyler," he mouthed.

Jessica wrenched the phone out of Neil's hands. "Tyler?" She tried to sound calm and composed. "Hey, what's happening?"

"That depends on you." His deep voice floated over the phone. "Are you free for dinner?"

"Hmmm." Jessica paused, her mind working furiously. Dating 101 said that you were always busy if a guy called to ask you out on the same day. *But I really want to see him,* Jessica thought. *Oh, well, who cares? I'd rather have dinner with him than sit at home and watch Sam channel surf while Liz doesn't yell at him for doing it.*

"That depends on where you're taking me," Jessica responded.

"How about this really cool new Japanese place?" he suggested. "Are you into that?"

"I love Japanese," Jessica said enthusiastically. Delicious, low cal, and sophisticated—what more could you ask for?

"How's eight?" Tyler asked. "I'll pick you up."

"Sounds perfect." Jessica smiled into the phone. She couldn't remember the last time she'd been this excited about going out to dinner with a guy. She gave him directions to the house, hung up the phone, and spun around to face Neil.

"Yo." Neil high-fived her. "You owe me five bucks."

"Omigod!" Jessica paled. "I've got nothing to wear! All my good stuff is at the cleaner's! What am I going to do?"

"Borrow something from Elizabeth?" Neil suggested.

"Yeah, like chinos and an oxford shirt are really cutting edge, Neil," Jessica complained, frowning. "Of course, now that Liz is so into Sam, she is dressing a little better."

"Yeah, didn't I see her showing you some dress she'd just bought the other day?"

"You're right! It's totally cute. Okay, gotta raid my sister's closet. I'll see you later, Neil." Jessica kissed him on the cheek and bounded out of the kitchen.

Jessica flew up the two flights of stairs to Elizabeth's attic room. She poked her head inside. The coast was clear. She slipped in and closed the door quietly behind her, then dashed to the closet.

"Perfect," Jessica said admiringly as she took out the sundress and smoothed its folds. It was much cuter than Elizabeth's usual style. Little pink flowers all over a black background. Jessica held it against herself and walked over to the mirror.

Maybe those little daisy earrings would work

with this, she thought, dropping the dress on Elizabeth's neatly made bed and walking over to her dresser. She opened the top drawer and began rooting around for the small box that Elizabeth kept her earrings in.

What's this? Jessica wondered as her gaze landed on an envelope from the University of London. It lay half covered by Elizabeth's journal, which Jessica knew better than to peek at. But she couldn't help snooping into the letter.

We wish to extend our congratulations on your being accepted to the visiting-writers program for the fall semester at the University of London. . . .

"Whaa?" Jessica fell back on the bed, the letter clutched tightly in her hand. "London? As in England! Fall semester? What's going on?"

Jessica stared at the letter again, her mind racing as she considered what it could mean.

Okay, so Elizabeth was accepted into this obviously way fab writing program at some English university—a London university!—that's not so hard to figure out. But why didn't she say anything about it?

Because she's going to turn it down. The thought slammed into Jessica's head. *She's going to turn it down so she can stay in Sweet Valley and be with that cheating slacker Sam.*

Jessica paled at the thought. Elizabeth's whole life was about becoming a writer. Jessica couldn't stand by and watch her throw away her dream so easily. It was one thing to take the summer off. It was quite another to turn down something like this. The University of London was really prestigious. Even Jessica had heard of it! How could Elizabeth turn down a semester abroad to hang out at the beach with Sam?

Jessica got up and began pacing nervously around the room. She knew she had to stop Elizabeth, but how? A flash of pink caught her eye as she passed the window, and she stopped to peer out.

Elizabeth! She was sitting on the lawn, sunning herself in a pink halter and teeny white shorts. *Hey, it looks like she's been borrowing* my *clothes,* Jessica thought, momentarily distracted. She stared at Elizabeth, a plan forming itself in her mind.

She knew that she couldn't tell Elizabeth that she'd been snooping through her things, but maybe she could join Elizabeth on the lawn, get her talking, and steer the conversation in such a way that the subject of London just came up naturally. . . .

That's it, Jessica thought, nodding decisively. She slipped the envelope half under the journal exactly as she'd found it, then marched out of the room, forgetting to take the sundress with her.

Jessica had more important things to worry about than what to wear on her upcoming date. She was too busy figuring out how to stop her sister from ruining her life.

Sam lay on his back in bed and stared listlessly at the ceiling. He knew that he should motivate and get out of bed. But he really didn't want to. Because once he got out of bed, he'd have to start dealing with things—like whether he should call Julia back and tell her that he was going to the wedding. Or not going. Or going. Or not.

Man, oh, man!

He should have called her already, but he still hadn't made up his mind about what to do. If he *did* go to the wedding, he'd be knee-deep in family hassles. If he *didn't* go to the wedding, he'd seriously hurt Julia, and he really didn't want to do that.

Sam exhaled in frustration as he considered the possibilities and came up with the inescapable conclusion that whichever way he decided, he'd be screwed.

He rolled over and reached under the bed, rooting around until he found what he was looking for. His hand closed over a dusty leather book, and he dragged it out and plunked it on his lap.

Sam traced the gold lettering on the cover—

Photo Album. Although he hadn't talked to his family in two years, he couldn't bring himself to completely toss out all his reminders of them. Sam hadn't looked at his mother's face in months, and he felt strangely nervous. His hand trembled a little as he flipped open the book.

Neil pushed open the door and poked his head inside. "Hey, can I come in a sec?"

Sam was startled by the interruption, and he quickly closed the photo album. "What's up?"

"Just wondering if I could borrow some shaving cream," Neil said, rubbing his morning stubble.

"Over there—" Sam nodded toward his dresser. "There should be a can somewhere around."

Neil sifted through the mess on Sam's dresser. "Thanks, bud. I use this kind," he said, tossing the can up in the air and catching it. He stared at the album in Sam's hand. "I didn't even know you had a photo album. Not family, I assume."

"Actually, yes." Sam paused. He opened the book and pointed to a photograph of a cute girl eating a hot dog and wearing a baseball cap. "This is my cousin Julia, the one I was telling you about."

"Hey, I never envisioned you as the outdoors type," Neil said as he sat down next to Sam, his eyes on a picture of Sam and Julia hiking.

"I'm not," Sam said, glancing at the photo. It had been taken about four or five years ago. "But camping is, like, an approved activity according to my father. See this picture?" He tapped a shot of a guy wearing a paint-splattered shirt and standing in front of an easel with a goofy grin on his face. "That's my brother, Morgan."

"Yeah, I can see the resemblance," Neil said. "So he's into painting, huh?"

"*Was* into painting," Sam said bitterly. "My father wouldn't 'permit' such behavior from a Burgess. Not *manly* enough. Not *corporate* enough."

"I know the name of that tune," Neil said quietly.

Sam shot Neil a sidelong glance. Was he treading on sensitive ground here? Neil had become a good buddy, and Sam knew that he'd had his own share of family problems after coming out of the closet.

Neil shook his head. "I could build an entire house brick by brick with my own two hands and still not be 'manly' enough for my father. *Gay* means *freak* in their minds."

Sam gave Neil an empathetic look. "Family sure can suck."

Neil nodded, flipping another page in the album.

"My dad just couldn't deal with the fact that Morgan had his own dreams," Sam said. "Dad can't stand anything sensitive or creative. Painting just doesn't cut it. Camping, fishing, those are okay things to do."

"So Morgan took off like you, huh?" Neil asked.

"Are you kidding?" Sam laughed bitterly. "Forget that. Morgan, like, totally buckled down and became a corporate drone in the Burgess empire. Now he's as bad as my father. That's part of why I got out—I figured that if I didn't, I'd end up like Morgan. Just the thought of seeing both of them at the wedding gives me the heebie-jeebies."

Neil leafed through the album. "I can understand that. But what about her?" He pointed to a picture of Julia and Sam with their arms around each other. "How about going to the wedding just to see Julia?"

"I don't know," Sam said. "I am really crazy about Jules. Always have been. See this picture of me with the big striped bass? I was about fourteen, and we were all on this fishing trip, and my dad was really ragging me about not catching anything." His smile faded at the memory. "So Julia tells him that she knows this great place, teeming with fish. She's gonna take me up there and teach me how to fish. She's sure that we'll catch dinner for the whole family." Sam paused and shook his head.

"So what happened?" Neil prodded.

"It was great," Sam said. "We went to this really secluded spot and just kicked back. Julia could tell I needed to get the hell away from them for a while. She's older than I am, and she told me a lot of stuff about what college would be like. I remember I kept asking her advice on how to kiss girls."

"Yeah? What did she say?" Neil quirked an eyebrow.

"Mainly she told me how important it was to respect women," Sam said. "Not to pressure them and also not to use too much saliva." Sam laughed. "But anyway, after a couple of hours she baited a hook, cast off, and caught this mother." He pointed to the bass. "When we joined the rest of the family, Julia told everyone that I'd caught it. It may sound like no big deal, but when you're fourteen and your hormones are working overtime and your dad and brother are constantly trying to undermine your confidence, a little kindness helps. Helps a lot."

"Seems like asking you to the wedding is a pretty small favor compared to some of the stuff she's done for you," Neil commented.

"You're right." Sam closed the album and shoved it back under the bed. "But I just can't stand the thought of coming face-to-face with my old man over the shrimp cocktail."

"You know," Neil said slowly, "maybe you're thinking about this the wrong way. I mean, just suppose you went—don't you think it might feel great to show your parents that you've been able to make it without their help? Without having to play by their rules and live off your trust fund? I don't know about you." Neil tossed the can of shaving cream up in the air. "But I'd love to be able to show my parents that."

Sam looked thoughtful. "You may have a point. And I would really like to see Julia too."

"So then go," Neil urged. "Just go and have a great time."

"Yeah, well, there's one other problem with that," Sam said. "Just how am I going to show my parents that I can survive without them when I don't even have the bucks to get to Boston?" He ran his hands through his hair in frustration. "So thanks for helping me figure things out, Neil, but unless I win the lottery overnight, looks like I'm gonna have to tell Julia that I'm a no-show."

Elizabeth closed her eyes and leaned against the side of the house with her legs stretched out in front of her. She could hardly believe she was wearing a pair of shorts so teeny. Or that she was also wearing a hot pink halter. If anyone walked by and spotted her, she would definitely be mistaken for Jessica.

Was it so wrong to want to look sexy for her boyfriend? It wasn't like she could hang around the house in her rattiest, baggiest clothes for comfort. She lived with Sam!

Elizabeth closed her eyes and smiled up at the sun, which felt heavenly on her bare skin. Lying out was a treat, especially after the night she'd had. She'd tossed and turned, stressing about what she was going to do about the scholarship to the University of London. She knew that she didn't want to go, but she also knew that she shouldn't turn them down. A semester abroad. Who turned that down? No one!

Of course, the decision to turn them down would be easier if things were going a little more smoothly with Sam. It's not that things weren't good. And it's not that she didn't expect to have a great summer with him. In fact, she figured that by the end of the summer, their relationship would be cemented, all the kinks worked out.

And then she'd leave for months? Just when she'd gotten the relationship she'd always wanted?

Just when Sam had gotten used to having a serious girlfriend? Used to commitment?

Sam. Elizabeth sighed. What was the deal there? He'd practically run away from her on campus yesterday and hadn't come back until late at night. Was he deliberately avoiding her? She didn't like to think about the fact that he'd seemed kind of distant ever since she'd told him that she was ready to make love.

It's so ironic, Elizabeth thought, exhaling gustily as she rubbed sunblock on her legs, *that when I'm finally ready to sleep with a guy, he doesn't want to. Come on,* she told herself. *You know it's not that he doesn't want to. He wants to. He's simply thinking of you.* She tossed the tube of sunblock on the grass and reached for her glass of iced tea.

"Hey, Liz. Busy?"

Elizabeth squinted to see Jessica, in her own teeny shorts and tank top, plopping down on the grass beside her. "Do I look busy?" she asked, grinning. "Although if you're gonna start dissing Sam, I *am* busy. So save your breath."

"What makes you think I want to diss Sam?" Jessica asked, not even trying to mock confusion. She picked up Elizabeth's glass and took a long swig.

"Gee, I don't know," Elizabeth said. "I mean, it couldn't be the fact that the last five times we've talked, you've told me that he isn't good enough for me, could it?"

"Oh, Lizzie." Jessica reached for the sunblock. "Can't you just see that I'm looking out for you? Besides"—she smoothed some of the cream on her arms—"it's your life, right? If you want Sam as your boyfriend, that's your business. I know why you like him, Liz."

"Oh, really?" Elizabeth asked.

"He's gorgeous, for one," Jessica admitted, lying back on the grass. "And when he's not lying about something or being a jerk, he can be really cool."

Elizabeth rolled her eyes. "How nice of you, Jess." She plucked her iced-tea glass out of Jessica's hand and took a sip.

"No, really." Jessica nodded. "I mean, if you'd actually give up a semester abroad for Sam, he's gotta be the most amazing boyfriend a girl could have."

Elizabeth practically spit out the iced tea. She bolted up and grabbed Jessica's hand. "How do you know about that?"

Jessica avoided Elizabeth's furious glare. "I'm not even going to lie. I was in your room, looking for an outfit to borrow, and I saw the envelope from the University of London on your desk. I got curious, so I looked. I'm not even sorry about it."

"Well, you should be!" Elizabeth said. "How dare you snoop in my private stuff? I can't believe—"

"Look, Elizabeth," Jessica said, sitting up. "If you were going to accept that scholarship, you would have been dancing all over the house. So, I figure you're turning it down. And the only reason that you'd turn down something as fab as that is because you've managed to convince yourself that Sam's worth it. Well, trust me. He isn't. A semester in London? How could you choose Sam over that?"

Elizabeth's cheeks flamed. "First of all, how dare you look through my stuff?" She dabbed at the splotches of tea that now decorated the front of her halter. "Second of all—"

"Forget the stupid snooping," Jessica insisted. "I already said I wasn't sorry. And I'm not. Let's deal with the real issues here, not the petty stuff. How can you give up your dream for that slacker?"

"I don't consider you going through my things just some *petty* stuff," Elizabeth said stiffly. "But you're right; that's not the point."

"So what's the point?" Jessica snapped. "That it's none of my business? Right. Like I'm not your twin. Like I don't care that you're throwing away your life."

Elizabeth didn't know what to say. She was beyond upset that Jessica had outed her, and she couldn't stand the way her sister talked about Sam. Still, she was happy that she could share her secret with her twin. It would certainly make things easier if she could talk about her situation with *someone*.

If only Jess was a little less biased against Sam, Elizabeth thought, sighing. "Listen, let's just get this one straight, okay? I do *not* appreciate your going through my things. And who said you could borrow my sundress anyway? But just so you know, I haven't decided to give up on the scholarship. I just haven't mentioned it because I need time to think about it."

"Well, that's a relief," Jessica said. "It would totally blow if you were going to give up some major writing scholarship just because you were afraid to leave your boyfriend."

"Uh, Jessica?" Elizabeth bit out, frustration evident. "I don't think you heard me correctly. I didn't say that I was going. I just said that I needed some time to think."

"What do you need to think about?" Jessica asked in amazement. She looked at her sister like she was crazy. "The guy's cute, Liz. I get it, okay? But he's not worth you. He couldn't even handle a kiss! He took off after that, or don't you remember? You had to go hunting him down, and where do you find him? Shacked up with a girl in the ritziest hotel in Sweet Valley. Which his parents just so happen to own? Surprise after surprise."

"Jess, that girl was his platonic friend Anna," Elizabeth said, weary of defending him, defending herself, defending her choice to be with him. "And yeah, that all sounds pretty bad when you put it that way. But Sam has explained himself to me, and

I'm the one who has to accept it or not. And I choose to. Okay? It's taken me and Sam a long time to get to this point. Sam's a really incredible guy. He's got some issues, yes. I'm aware of them, believe me."

Jessica shook her head. "Before you two hooked up, you weren't even speaking to Sam for, like, two months! He took off on you after a kiss, then he comes home, you give him the cold shoulder, and he accepts it. He doesn't even try to make things right!"

Elizabeth felt her anger getting hotter. "Jess, he did try. *I* shut him out. *I* wouldn't talk to him. *I* wouldn't let him explain. I was too angry. But anyway, enough already! This isn't your business!"

"I'm sick of him using all my food!" Jessica shouted. "He didn't even replace my skim milk after he finished it the other day!"

Elizabeth glared at her. "Oh, like that is such a major war crime." She stood up and began to gather her sunblock and iced-tea glass. "I mean, you're absolutely right, Jessica—I should *definitely* go to another country to get away from a monster like that." She shook her head in disgust. "Unless you can come up with something better than that, don't even bother talking to me about this." Elizabeth marched into the house, banging the door behind her.

Chapter
Five

Tyler whistled appreciatively. "Wow, great dress."

"Thanks!" Jessica smiled. She knew she looked terrific in Elizabeth's dress. The black was striking against her tan, and the pink flowers added a feminine quality Jessica loved. Tyler was looking pretty cute too, in black jeans and a black T-shirt that emphasized his lanky yet muscular build.

"So this place is just a few blocks from here," Tyler said, taking her arm as they set off down the sidewalk. "I figured we could walk."

Jessica nodded agreeably. She could manage at least a few blocks in her heels; the important thing was the fact that Tyler was holding her arm!

"So this is it," Tyler said. He gestured toward a flight of stairs that led down to a tiny door covered in cherry blossoms. They headed down and walked inside.

"Wow, this is great." Jessica looked around as a kimono-clad hostess led them to a table. The restaurant was totally romantic, with soft lighting coming from rice-paper lanterns and the seductive sound of Japanese wooden flutes floating through the air.

Tyler's so sophisticated, Jessica thought as she sat down. Her last date had taken her to a burrito hut on the boardwalk.

"How about some California rolls and sake?" Tyler looked at her over the edge of his menu. "Sound good?"

"Sounds terrific." Jessica put down her menu and smiled at him.

"So how's it going at Yum-Yums?" Tyler asked after he'd given the waitress their order. "Are they cool about extending your hours?"

"Yeah, pretty cool." Jessica toyed with her water glass. "I guess it's okay. I don't want to complain, but it's not exactly the most challenging job. Not like what you have going at the gallery," she added wistfully.

"Hey," Tyler said, laughing. "The gallery isn't all that challenging. I spend a lot of time hanging around the fax machine, making sure that it's stocked with paper."

"Still," Jessica persisted. "You know what you want in life, and you're immersing yourself in the right environment. I just feel like I'm floating. I thought I knew what I wanted out of life, but now I'm not sure."

Tyler looked thoughtful. "You should stop seeing that as a problem and start seeing it as a really cool thing."

"How?" Jessica was intrigued. She couldn't get over how comfortable she felt with Tyler or how considerate he was. He seemed truly interested in her problems.

"Well, like I said when we met—" Tyler paused as the waitress set down their order. "You're in a really open place right now. You're not locked into anything; it's all before you. There's real freedom in that."

"That's true." Jessica took a sip of her sake. "This is delicious." She'd never tasted anything like the slightly sweet, tangy flavor of the rice wine.

"My sister's stressing over the same things right now," Tyler continued, biting into a California roll. "She's freaked out because she's graduating from high school next week, and she doesn't know what she wants to major in at college."

"Yeah, but that's, like, normal when you're in high school," Jessica said in dismay. "I'm going to be a *junior* in the fall!"

"Hey, everyone has their own schedule," Tyler said. "What's the rush? Experiment. When you find what's right for you, you'll know."

Jessica took another sip of the sake. "I thought I'd found it when I started taking art history. But I don't know—I find it interesting, but not *fascinating*. Is that what painting is for you?" She looked at Tyler inquisitively. "Fascinating?"

Tyler nodded in understanding. "Sometimes. But sometimes it's frustrating as hell. It depends on the day. Or actually, if I'm being honest, it depends on how well I'm painting at any given time."

"And when you're painting well?" Jessica asked. She was mesmerized by the sparkle in Tyler's deep gray eyes. He was so good-looking, so interesting, so . . . *everything*.

Tyler's gorgeous face lit up. "When I'm painting well, I feel like I'm on top of the world. It's like this totally magical thing to capture something beautiful and get it right. Get it so you know that your vision comes across loud and clear to the viewer." He paused for a second and looked shy. "You know what?" he asked quietly.

"What?" Jessica asked. She'd never seen a guy speak so passionately about anything, and she was totally captivated by the depths of Tyler's passion.

"Well, about capturing something beautiful,"

he said. "I'd love to paint you, Jessica."

Jessica felt like her whole body was on fire. She couldn't remember the last time a guy had this kind of effect on her. She was sure she'd never talked as openly and directly about her hopes and fears before. Well, maybe with Neil or her sister, but that wasn't the same thing.

She gazed at Tyler in the soft light, struck by how gorgeous he looked with the lanterns casting mysterious shadows on his face. *He's the one that should be painted,* she thought. Still, she wasn't about to turn down the opportunity of having him paint her. She couldn't imagine how thrilling it would be to see herself brought to life by his brush. "I—I would be honored," she finally managed to stammer.

"No," Tyler said softly, reaching across the table to take her hand. "I'm the one who'd be honored, Jessica."

And with that, Jessica Wakefield fell totally in love.

"Wanna order in some Chinese?" Sam asked lazily. He was lying on his bed with Elizabeth, and he didn't feel up to making dinner or going out. He had just about enough energy to punch some numbers into the phone. Well, maybe he could make it to the door and pay the delivery guy, but he wasn't up for much more than that.

"Um, maybe," Elizabeth said, burrowing even deeper into the circle of his arms. "I'm not really that hungry. I just kind of want to hang out and talk, okay?"

"Sure," Sam said. He stroked her hair with one hand, amazed at how silky it was. Sometimes he was just so blown away by how beautiful she was. "What's on your mind?"

"I was wondering if you've made up your mind about the wedding," Elizabeth said quietly. She raised her head and looked Sam in the eyes. "I mean, I know it's a really tough decision for you. . . ."

Sam exhaled noisily. "Yeah," he said in a clipped voice. He wasn't into talking about it, but he couldn't help being touched by how thoughtful Elizabeth was. "I've thought about it, and I guess I'd like to go." He ran a hand through his hair. "I'd be psyched to see Julia, but it's not that simple."

"Oh, Sam, why not?" Elizabeth bounced up on the bed excitedly. "It would be so great!"

"Yeah, it might be," Sam agreed, rolling over to reach under the bed for the photo album. He couldn't believe that he was showing it to so many people. First Neil, now Elizabeth . . .

"Wanna see a picture of Julia?" he asked her.

"Are you kidding? I'd love to!"

Sam flipped the book open to a shot of him and Julia pitching a tent. "This is from when we used to go camping every summer."

"She's pretty," Elizabeth said, peering over his shoulder. "She looks like you, sort of."

Sam studied the photograph. "Yeah, she does in a way. You know, I never noticed that before. It's weird—I mean, in a lot of ways I always felt closer to her than I did to Morgan."

Damn, I miss Jules, he thought, swallowing hard. He was suddenly overcome by emotion and turned his head away from Elizabeth. He was embarrassed by how choked up he was getting. But Elizabeth was being tactfully silent, engrossed in the pictures, and Sam was grateful that she was distracted.

He was also grateful that she didn't ask questions about the other people in the photos, about his parents or brother. When she turned the last page, Sam closed the album, relieved to put it away.

"It would be great to go," he said. "I'd even risk dealing with my parents again for Julia, but . . ." Sam trailed off and shook his head.

"But what?" Elizabeth asked.

"Cash," Sam explained. "I don't have the bucks to fly to Boston right now. About the only way I could get there would be to walk."

"Oh, Sam." Elizabeth looked crestfallen. "I'm really sorry."

"Yeah, well, what can I do?" He tried to laugh it off. "Listen, how about that Chinese?" Sam raised his eyebrows. Elizabeth had a far-off look on her face, and she didn't seem to be listening to him. "Liz?"

"I've got it!" Elizabeth jumped up, the photo album toppling to the floor. "Sam, I have got the most fabulous, brilliant, romantic idea!" She spun around with a look of pure joy.

"Okay," he said, picking up the album. "Wanna let me in on it?"

"We'll drive cross-country!" Elizabeth exclaimed. "A road trip! Oh, Sam, it will be so perfect!"

"Uh, back up a little, Elizabeth." Sam held up his hand. "A road trip? Like that doesn't cost money? What about a car?"

"The Jeep," Elizabeth said triumphantly, her eyes sparkling with happiness. "Jess and I are supposed to share it, but since she doesn't need it for work at Yum-Yums, I'm sure she'll let us take it for a couple of weeks."

"I don't know, Liz," Sam said. "What about gas, hotel bills. . . ."

Elizabeth was beaming. "I'll chip in for the gas, and who said anything about hotels? We'll stay in little roadside dives!"

Sam had to admit that Elizabeth was making sense, but something didn't sound right, and he couldn't put his finger on it.

"We'll have a great time," Elizabeth went on excitedly. "We'll take the scenic route—it'll probably take two weeks there and back. We'll see the entire country!"

She continued chattering away excitedly, but Sam realized he was tuning her out. He'd figured out what exactly didn't sound right.

We'll *drive cross-country*? We'll *have a great time*? *Since when did this become a trip for two*?

He stared at Elizabeth, aghast, imagining the implications of her meeting his parents. But how would he get to Julia's wedding unless he drove with her? And she did have a point about a road trip being fun . . .

Dude, have you gone crazy? Sam shook his head. *Two weeks in a car and then she meets my family? Our relationship will, like, take a warp jump!*

"Say yes, Sam, please?" Elizabeth looked at him pleadingly.

"Well . . ." Sam didn't know what to do. It was definitely the only chance he had to get to the wedding, and he did hate to disappoint Elizabeth. . . . "Okay." He nodded, as if convincing himself it was a good idea. "Let's do it."

What am I getting myself into? he wondered.

We'll be together 24/7 for a couple of weeks, then we'll end up at the wedding, and she'll meet my family. What comes after that? Sam thought as Elizabeth threw her arms around him. *A double wedding?*

"Hey, Jess, the cappuccino machine had a total fit," Liza, Yum-Yums' assistant manager, said as she filled the sugar dispensers. "It exploded all over the counter. Do you think you could clean it up and then check the steamer attachment and see why it blew?"

Jessica smiled. "Sure thing." She dropped her bag behind the counter and grabbed an apron. She was working the early shift at Yums, and though ordinarily that would have been enough to put her in a bad mood, *nothing* could wipe the smile off her face this morning.

"Are you kidding?" Liza asked, watching Jessica swipe down the sticky foam that had congealed on the marble countertops. "That's your least-favorite job. You usually bitch for hours when I ask you to fix the machine."

"That's true," Jessica said, grinning. "But that was before I found out that my sister and her slacker boyfriend are going to be out of my hair for the next two weeks."

Liza laughed. "Hey—I thought you and

Elizabeth were practically best friends."

"Yeah, sure, I love Elizabeth," Jessica explained. "It's her boyfriend I'm not so crazy about." Jessica fiddled with the steam attachment. "No Sam for two weeks? No Elizabeth and Sam sucking face all over the house for two weeks? Yup—I could go for that."

Liza chuckled. "Is he really that bad? I mean, Elizabeth seems pretty smart. Why is she hanging with such a loser?"

"It's not that he's a loser, exactly," Jessica admitted reluctantly. "He's really smart, incredibly good-looking, and kind of funny too. . . ."

Liza raised her eyebrows. "If that's your idea of a bad boyfriend, do you think you could fix me up with some of your rejects?"

"Trust me," Jessica began. "He's also, like, totally immature, he's a slacker, and even worse, I don't trust him. Not one bit." Jessica paused for a second. "He cares about Elizabeth, but he puts on the brakes. Know what I mean? I'm just afraid she'll get hurt. Really hurt. Listen, enough about Sam. Can I take a break? I really need a cup of coffee myself. I know I've only been here, like, ten minutes, but I should get bonus points for fixing the machine."

Liza laughed. "Go ahead."

Jessica whipped off her apron and helped herself

to a chocolate croissant and a mochaccino. The place was just starting to fill up, so she grabbed a quiet corner booth before anyone else could take it. She leaned back and took a sip of her mochaccino, savoring the combination of steamed milk and cinnamon.

She closed her eyes as she replayed the events of the past two days. What had seemed like the beginning of a truly sucky summer was shaping up pretty nicely. Yums was an okay place to work; Tyler was definitely a superhot prospect, and best of all, she was going to get a break from Sam.

"Hey, can I sit down, or would I be interrupting some kind of trance or something?"

"Neil!" Jessica's eyes flew open. "Have you heard the good news?"

Neil sat down next to her, his own mochaccino and a blueberry muffin on a tray. "Man! I thought I was gonna tell you. How'd you hear? I thought you were gone before the lovebirds woke up."

Jessica stole a tiny piece of Neil's muffin. "I went to return Liz's sundress this morning, and she told me all about it."

"Ah," Neil said. "Hey, guess what? Turns out I have to leave tomorrow morning for my camp job. They need me to help set up the whole sports program."

Jessica's heart sank. That was terrible news! She

slumped against the back of the booth.

Neil eyed her. "Why do you look like you just—"

"Lost my best friend?" Jessica supplied. "Because I did. Think about it, Neil, I'm going to be totally alone! Liz is leaving, you're leaving, and all my girlfriends are already gone! I'm gonna be totally alone here!"

"What about Tyler?" Neil asked. "He'll be around."

Jessica smiled. "That's true."

"And something tells me that with the rest of us out of the house, your relationship with Tyler is about to move at maximum warp."

"You know something, Neil?" Jessica took a bite of her croissant. She closed her eyes and conjured up an image of Tyler's gorgeous face. "You may have hit on something. No Liz, no Sam, no you, no hassles. Just me and Tyler and the whole house to ourselves. And to think"—she giggled—"just the other day I was worried about whether I was going to have a good summer or not!"

Chapter Six

"I know Santa Fe is a little out of the way, but not really," Elizabeth said as she began marking the route on the map with a yellow highlighter.

"What do you mean, not really out of the way?" Sam asked suspiciously. He pulled his baseball cap around so that the bill was in front and gave Elizabeth a sidelong glance.

"I mean," Elizabeth said slowly, "that it's not the most direct route, but it *does* follow the major highway, so it will actually be faster." She looked up from the map and smiled at Sam.

They'd been sitting in the kitchen for the last hour, trying to figure out the most efficient route to Boston, and Elizabeth was growing more excited by the second. *This is going to be fabulous,* she thought dreamily. *It'll be so romantic!*

"What are you smiling about?" Sam leaned

forward and tucked a lock of Elizabeth's hair behind her ear. "You looked all rosy for a second."

"Oh, I was just thinking about the way we met," Elizabeth said. "It was almost exactly a year ago, Sam. On a cross-country road trip. It's like fate that we're doing it again—this time as a couple!"

Sam nodded and planted a kiss on her cheek. "It'll be a blast."

"Oh, c'mon, Sam. It's going to be a lot more than that," Elizabeth insisted. "It's going to be totally fabulous." She paused for a second, unsure of how to say what she wanted. Sometimes Sam could be so touchy, especially when it came to his family, but she wanted to tell him how much the trip meant to her, how much it could mean for both of them.

"Sam." Elizabeth reached out for his hand.

"What?" Sam squeezed her hand and gave her a small smile. It was a smile that Elizabeth had seen before. Sam looked at her like she was the most beautiful girl in the world, like she was the most fragile flower. Ordinarily Elizabeth wouldn't have liked to be thought of in those terms, but there was something so incredibly special about cynical Sam regarding her so tenderly. Elizabeth was sure that if Jessica could see the depth of feeling in his eyes, she would totally change her opinion of him.

105

Elizabeth caressed his chin. "I was thinking that this wedding could be just the thing that could get your relationship with your parents back on track. After all, it's going to be a really festive occasion, everyone will be in really high spirits. . . ."

"Well, you're wrong," Sam said flatly, the light in his eyes fading abruptly. "Believe me, Liz, I'm going as a favor to Julia, but I'm going to try and avoid my parents as much as possible. And as far as it being a festive occasion—" He shook his head ruefully. "Trust me—about the only thing that makes my father crack a smile is a tax refund." Sam let go of her hand and got up to pace around the kitchen.

Elizabeth watched Sam silently for a few minutes with a small frown on her face. It was amazing the way he could morph from a totally tender boyfriend into a cold, indifferent guy in a matter of seconds. That's the way the rest of the world saw him, but Elizabeth never forgot what was underneath the facade, and she was sure that if he made up with his parents, the tough exterior would completely melt away.

I know that when Sam sees them again, he'll feel differently, Elizabeth reassured herself. She knew that she was right, but she also knew when not to push. They had the whole trip to talk about the reunion. With a sigh she turned back to the table and reached for her date book. "Well, look," Elizabeth said cheerfully. "We've pretty much finished marking out the route. I'm going to make a shopping list. Do you think you could hit the drugstore for me?"

"Yeah, sure," Sam said. "Whaddya want?"

"We definitely need toothpaste," Elizabeth said, scribbling a list. "Um, sunblock for sure, insect repellent—how about a first-aid kit?" She looked at Sam quizzically.

"Liz, we're going to be driving from so-Cal to Cambridge, not hiking in Death Valley."

"Well, I just want to be prepared," Elizabeth protested.

"Okay, I'll get the stuff." Sam crouched by her chair and reached for the list. "Listen, Liz, we're going to have a great time. You're right. It will be like when we met."

"Only this time we won't be driving each other crazy the whole time," Elizabeth said happily.

"We won't?" Sam gave her a lazy grin. "I've got news for you, Elizabeth." He moved his face so close to hers that she could feel his warm breath tickle her cheek. "You drive me crazy *all* the time." He bent his head to kiss her.

"Hmmm," Elizabeth whispered. "You better get going, Sam. 'Cause if you don't leave now, I won't let you go for hours."

Sam grinned as he scooped up the list and shoved it into his back pocket. "That wouldn't be the worst thing. See you later." He winked at her.

Elizabeth leaned back against her chair and watched him leave with a small smile on her face. She was sure that driving to Boston with Sam was just what their relationship needed. They'd be together 24/7 without any distractions, and they'd come back an even closer couple than before.

Really close, Elizabeth thought as she gathered up her supplies and folded away the map. After all, hadn't Sam said that he thought they needed more time before they made love? Elizabeth giggled. *Well, except for taking a slow boat to China, I can't think of many things that would take more time than driving cross-country!*

Jessica whistled a jaunty tune as she busied herself with wiping down the counter and restocking the napkin holders. Yums was practically empty, and there weren't any customers clamoring for her attention, so she was free to daydream about Tyler.

Their date the night before had been way beyond awesome, and she hadn't been able to think about anything else since she'd woken up.

Where would they go next time? Because there was obviously going to be a next time. She'd never felt as sure of anything in her whole life.

Maybe he'll paint me on our next date, Jessica thought happily. *Maybe we'll—*

"Tyler!" she exclaimed as the object of her daydreams walked in. He looked great, even better than the night before, in a pair of paint-splattered cargo pants and a formfitting T-shirt.

"Hey, Jessica," Tyler murmured as he bent to kiss her cheek. He gave her a brief smile, but he seemed a little distracted.

"Is something wrong?" Jessica asked in concern.

"Nothing too serious, just a couple of unforeseen hassles," Tyler said, running a hand through his hair. "Remember I told you that my sister's graduating from high school? My ride fell through, and now there's no way I can get there. I definitely can't afford a plane ticket to Illinois." He unrolled a sheaf of papers that he'd been carrying under his arm and showed them to Jessica.

She read one of the flyers: "Going east? I'll pay all gas and tolls to Illinois."

Tyler's leaving? First Elizabeth, then Neil, now Tyler! Perfect! She sighed heavily. Oh, well, she could always hang around Sweet Valley by herself, maybe even take on some *more* hours at Yums. . . . *Yeah, and I could pierce my nose and shave my head too.* Jessica felt like crying. Nothing was worse than meeting the perfect guy

109

and then having him vanish like a puff of smoke!

"I better get these posted around town," he said, worry marring his perfect features. "Unless you mysteriously know someone who's heading east in the next day or two, I'm in—"

Hello! Where have I been living? Jessica shook her head in disbelief. *Of course* she knew someone who was driving east! Why even stress for a second? She had the perfect answer to all their problems!

She could help Tyler get to his sister's graduation *and* help put their relationship on the fast track—nothing was guaranteed to shift things into high gear more than a road trip complete with overnight motel pit stops.

"You know, Tyler," she interrupted, "I may just be able to help you. My sister and her boyfriend are driving to Boston—they're leaving tomorrow! They'd be thrilled to have someone pay the gas and tolls for half of their trip."

I'm sure that's true, Jessica thought, crossing her fingers behind her back. "Not only that," she continued brightly. "But I was thinking of going with them."

"You were?" Now Tyler definitely looked interested.

Jessica nodded.

"That could work." Tyler scratched his chin thoughtfully.

Jessica noticed that he hadn't shaved that morning and that he looked even more gorgeous with a hint of stubble. *Imagine what it's going to be like being with him every waking minute,* she thought with a thrill. "Of course it could work!" she exclaimed. "It's perfect!"

"You're right!" Tyler grinned. "What can I say—you've saved my life, Jessica." He wadded up the flyers and shoved them in the trash.

"Look, I'll call you later with the details, all right?" Jessica said, whipping off her apron. She had a ton of stuff to do if she was going to be ready by tomorrow.

"Fantastic," Tyler said. "And you're sure that your sister and her boyfriend will be cool with this?"

"Of course," Jessica assured him. In fact, the more she thought about it, the more she realized that she was practically doing Elizabeth a favor. First of all, she'd be helping her to save on gas and tolls, and second of all . . . *I'll be able to point out every stupid little thing that Sam does for the entire trip. By the time we get to Boston, Liz will be dying to dump him! We can leave him in the dust, and Elizabeth and I will drive back to Sweet Valley alone. She'll be totally into accepting the semester-abroad scholarship to the University of London!*

"There isn't going to be any problem, Tyler," Jessica assured him with a smile. "Trust me. Now get out of here, and start packing!"

"Hey, Liza?" Jessica called as Tyler walked out the door with an excited smile. "I'm taking a break, okay?" She grabbed a pen and paper from beside the cash register and began scribbling some notes.

"Let's see, hair spray, a new sexy nightie, um . . . I should probably get some more shorts. . . . Um, I know I'm forgetting something." Jessica frowned as she examined the list. "What do I need to do? Oh, that's right!" Her brow cleared, and she started writing again. "Convince Elizabeth to let Tyler and me come with her and Sam across the country!"

Elizabeth leaned back and studied the route she'd marked. It seemed pretty good. It wasn't the most direct way from Sweet Valley to Boston; she'd planned for a few scenic side trips, but what was the point of driving cross-country if you didn't take time to enjoy the scenery?

"Liz! Liz! I've got the most fantastic news!"

Startled, Elizabeth looked up as Jessica burst into the kitchen.

"Well, from the look on your face, it must be something pretty awesome," Elizabeth agreed. "So what happened? Did you win the lottery or something?"

Jessica plunked herself down next to Elizabeth. "No, in fact, if anything, I'd say that *you* won the lottery."

"How's that?" Elizabeth looked at her suspiciously. Jessica had one of those expressions on her face, the kind that said she'd come up with a wild idea, the kind of idea that Elizabeth didn't always think was so great.

"How'd you like it if I could come up with a way for all of your gas and tolls to be paid half of the way to Boston?" Jessica said with a mysterious expression.

"I'd say that you were a miracle worker," Elizabeth replied.

"Great! Oh, I'm so glad!" Jessica jumped up and went over to the refrigerator. "I mean, I knew I had a fantastic idea." She opened the door and rooted around inside. "But I was a little worried that *you* wouldn't see it that way." She popped the top on a bottle of iced tea and took a long swig. "I can't wait to call Tyler."

"Uh, Jess?" Elizabeth frowned. *What's she talking about anyway?* She turned around in her chair to look at her sister. "Don't you think you're forgetting something here? Like *what* this idea is and *why* you have to call Tyler?"

"You're, like, such a stickler for details, Liz," Jessica said, sighing. She slammed the refrigerator shut with her foot and walked back to the table. "Okay, it's like this." She sat down and began playing with some wilted daisies in a small vase, avoiding her sister's eyes. "Tyler has to get to Illinois, like, five minutes ago. He had a ride, but it fell through, so he's willing to pay gas and tolls." Jessica babbled, barely stopping to take a breath. "I told him that you guys were going and that, um, I was going too, and he was totally psyched. I mean the whole thing works perfectly, Elizabeth. You have to see that!"

"Maybe you need to back up a little," Elizabeth said, unsure if she'd heard her sister correctly. "I mean, it would be great to have someone help with the cost, and there's no reason that Tyler *shouldn't* come with us, but Jess, you told him that *you* were going with us? When did that happen?"

"Um, I don't know." Jessica looked innocent. "Maybe since he told me he was looking for a ride halfway across the country?"

"You sure are a piece of work." Elizabeth laughed admiringly. "But what's going to happen after we drop him in Illinois? You're going to come all the way to Boston with us? And back again?" She closed her eyes, imagining Jessica and Sam together in a car for two weeks. "Jessica, it will be a nightmare! You and Sam will be at each other's throats the whole time!"

"No, we won't, Lizzie," Jessica said in her sweetest voice. "You'll see—this will be the best thing for me and Sam. I'll really get to know him, find out what makes him tick. We'll—"

"Oh, spare me the bull." Elizabeth held up her hand, but she was laughing. "Like you really care about what makes Sam tick! You want to know what makes *Tyler* tick!"

"Okay, busted," Jessica admitted. "But admit it, Liz, you could use the help with the gas and tolls, and it will be a lot of fun for *us*. I feel like we've barely seen each other in weeks. We'll have a great time catching up."

"That's true," Elizabeth said thoughtfully as she chewed on the cap of her highlighter. "Things have been so rushed with finals. It does seem like a while since we've really talked. Aside from you snapping about Sam, I mean."

"So we can come?" Jessica bit her lip nervously. "Please? I mean, I already sort of told Tyler—"

"That it was okay," Elizabeth finished. "In that case, I think I should make you sweat."

Jessica's eyes widened. She stared at Elizabeth, hope bursting from her face.

Elizabeth cocked her head. "Okay, you and Tyler can come."

"Fantastic!" Jessica flung her arms around her. "You'll see, Elizabeth, you won't regret it. We'll have the best time!"

I won't regret it, Elizabeth echoed mentally as she squeezed Jessica into a hug. *Well, maybe I'll regret it a little when I tell Sam and he wrings my neck!*

*　　*　　*

115

"I couldn't find the toothpaste you wanted in an economy size," Sam called out as he walked into the kitchen, bowed under by the weight of a dozen different bags. "Hey, Liz?" He thumped the bags down on the table, ignoring the way half of their contents spilled out and onto the floor.

Sam shoved back his baseball cap and pushed back through the kitchen door into the living room. "Elizabeth?" he yelled up the stairs. "I'm back."

"Coming," she called from her room.

"Listen, you better be happy with what I got," he said as she skipped down the stairs. " 'Cause no way am I going out there again. It's, like, way hot, and I already went to three different stores to get your stuff."

"Thanks, you're such a sweetheart. How do I look in this? Do you think your parents will go for it?" She spun around, incredibly radiant.

"You look gorgeous," Sam said huskily, reaching out for her.

"Hey, Liz, what shoes are you taking with that dress?" Jessica walked down the stairs, her arms overflowing with a jumble of cosmetics. "It would work perfectly with those ankle straps I'm thinking of bringing. If I let you borrow the shoes, would you lend me the dress? Tyler would love it, and we can have it dry-cleaned after we leave Illinois." She didn't wait for a reply and zoomed past them into the kitchen.

116

Tyler? Jessica? Illinois? Whoa! What happened to Elizabeth and Sam?

"Whaaa?" Sam pulled away from Elizabeth abruptly. "Did I just hear anything even remotely like what I think I heard? 'Cause if I did, things are going to get really—"

"Liz? Do you still have that black bikini?" Jessica asked as she bounded out of the kitchen. "The one with the push-up—oh. Hi, Sam. You need to go out again and get me some sunblock. Listen, Liz, do you think six bikinis are enough for a two-week road trip? I have to see if the elastic in my polka-dot one is shot." She took the stairs two at a time.

"Liz?" Sam said when the whirlwind had passed. "You know this morning when you said that you wanted to sleep with me, and I thought that I was dreaming? That was like a really, really *good* dream. Hearing Jessica say that she and Tyler are coming along with us? That's like a really, really *bad* dream. So, I'm waiting for you to tell me that I missed something, that your crazy sister is talking about some *other* road trip."

"Listen, Sam, it's not as bad as you think," Elizabeth told him.

"If I'm not dreaming, it's much, much worse than I can even imagine," Sam said. "Haven't you picked up on the fact that I'm not exactly Jessica's favorite person?" *And she's not exactly on my hit parade either,*

117

Sam added silently. "She'll spend the whole trip totally ragging on me. And who's this Tyler person anyway? How do we know what he/she/or it is even like? How do we know Tyler isn't just some random serial killer who's conned Jessica into giving him a free ride cross-country?" He shook his head in disgust.

"Sam, you're getting yourself worked up over nothing," Elizabeth said soothingly. "Tyler's working at that gallery Jessica applied to, and I happen to know for a fact that they screen all applicants *very* carefully. They share a database on serial killers with the FBI, and Tyler came up clean, okay?"

"Whatever," Sam said impatiently. "That still doesn't change the fact that I'm going to be stuck in a car with Jessica for two weeks!"

"Sam—" Elizabeth pursed her lips. "Don't you see it's much better this way?"

"Uh, no, actually, I *don't* see that, and you're going to have a hell of a time convincing me that driving across the country with Jessica is better than being alone with you!"

"First of all, Tyler's going to be chipping in for gas and stuff all the way to Illinois."

"I guess that works," Sam admitted grudgingly.

"Second of all, this is the perfect opportunity for you and Jessica to get to know each other better."

I already know everything I need to about Jessica, Sam thought, biting back the words with difficulty.

118

"She's so into Tyler that she won't even have time to be getting on your case," Elizabeth continued blithely. "It's the perfect no-pressure way for her to see what a really great guy you are."

"Maybe," Sam said thoughtfully. Elizabeth might have a point. Besides, having Jessica and Tyler along for the ride would take some of the pressure off him. Elizabeth would want to be with Jessica at least part of the time. *And who knows, maybe Tyler will be a cool enough guy to hang out with,* Sam reassured himself.

"Hey, Sam." Jessica stuck her head over the banister from the second-floor landing. "When you pick up the sunblock, do you think you could get me some hair conditioner too? I use this special volumizing one that's hard to find, but you should be able to get some if you drive around to a couple of stores."

"Sure, Jess," Sam said sarcastically through gritted teeth. "Do you want me to get you some mascara too?"

"Yeah, good idea," Jessica said. Sam couldn't tell whether she was joking, but maybe his brand of sarcasm was too sophisticated for her. "And see if you can get some . . ."

But Sam wasn't listening. He was too busy trying to figure out how a proposed visit to his favorite cousin had morphed into what looked like was going to be the road trip from hell.

Chapter
Seven

"C'mon, you guys, let's get this show on the road," Sam called out as he finished loading the back of the Jeep. "We were supposed to have left twenty minutes ago."

"You forgot this," Jessica said as she struggled out of the door, carrying what looked like a giant hatbox. Sam thought they'd stopped making things like that about fifty years ago.

"I don't know if it will fit, exactly." Sam scratched his head and looked at the Jeep, which was packed to overflowing. "Okay, okay, I'll make it fit," he said hastily when he saw the expression on Jessica's face.

He had to admit, though, except for the fact that she insisted on packing enough stuff to clothe an army, Jessica wasn't being as much of a pain as she *could* be. Not only that, but it was an unexpected bonus that her friend was going to help out with the expenses. *Maybe this whole thing will work after all,* he thought as he shoved the hatbox in the back.

"Liz? Are you ready?" Sam yelled. He only hoped that she didn't come out with something else to pack.

"Right here," Elizabeth answered, coming out the door and locking it behind her. "Jess and I have been so psyched for the trip that we totally forgot to call our parents and tell them we were taking off for a couple of weeks! So I just got off the phone with them. They think the trip sounds great."

Is she trying to spread some family-unity cheer on my behalf? Sam wondered. Whatever. All he knew was that she looked incredibly pretty in a turquoise sundress. He smiled at her. Now that they were finally on their way, he was surprised to realize that he was looking forward to the trip. He gave a final shove to the hatbox before walking around to the front of the Jeep.

"Okay, let's get going. I'll take the first shift," Sam said as he slid behind the wheel.

"How come I don't get to drive?" Jessica asked.

"You can drive later, Jess," Elizabeth said as she hooked her seat belt. "Believe me—" She laughed. "By the time we get to Boston, you'll be sick of driving."

Sam pulled away from their house, his shades on, the music turned up. Life was good.

"Stop! Make a right!" Jessica shouted.

"Okay, okay, I'm not deaf," Sam said, glaring at her in the rearview mirror. "Straight ahead till the third light, right?" he asked, repeating the directions she'd given him over breakfast.

"Right," she said. "Now turn left. Now right. Stop!" she shrieked. "That's Tyler! You're passing his house!"

"Okay, chill, Jess." Sam put the Jeep in reverse. "It's not like we're halfway across the country already."

"Hey, guys," Tyler said as he slung a small duffel bag in the back and hopped in beside Jessica. "I'm Tyler, and you're obviously Jess's twin." He extended his hand. "Sam, right?" Tyler smiled. "You guys are really saving my life here."

Hey, he might be okay, Sam thought, surprised. Based on the way Jessica had described Tyler this morning, Sam had been worried that he'd be driving cross-country with a terminally hip guy in need of a major attitude adjustment. But Tyler seemed like a pretty relaxed dude, Sam thought as he eyed him in the rearview mirror. Where was the Parisian-painter type that Jessica had been raving about?

It seemed like the situation was under control,

122

and Sam felt like he could relax a little. He reached across the front seats and squeezed Elizabeth's hand.

"Hey, since we didn't get off to such a late start, maybe we have time to stop for a picnic later?" Elizabeth looked at him hopefully over the top of her sunglasses.

"I don't know." Sam shrugged. "Let's see if we make good time, okay?"

"Oh, c'mon!" Jessica poked her head between the seats. "A picnic would be, like, so awesome! Let's do it!"

"Hey," Sam protested as he signaled to turn onto the off-ramp. "I'm not saying no; I'm just saying we don't have to plan everything out."

"Ha!" Jessica laughed. "If Elizabeth and I don't plan, we'll probably end up at a gas station, eating microwave burritos."

"What's wrong with microwave burritos?" Sam and Tyler said in unison as the car dissolved in laughter.

I'm going to be able to hang with this, Sam thought as he grinned at Tyler. *Tyler's cool, Jess is behaving, Liz is great. . . . I've got no problem! Who'd have thought?*

Jessica clapped her hands over her ears. She knew that she must look crazy, but she had to do something to shut out Elizabeth and Sam's endless bickering. They'd been driving for hours, and things were going fine except that Elizabeth and Sam couldn't seem to agree on what was the best route to take to the San Diego Zoo.

I mean, who cares which route we take? Jessica bit her lip in frustration. *Just as long as we get there in the end!* She'd been excited when they'd all agreed that the zoo would be a perfect place to stop for lunch, but that had been hours ago, and now she was just feeling tired and irritable.

"Sam, I told you we should have gotten off at the earlier exit." Elizabeth sounded exasperated.

"It doesn't make sense to get off the highway now. We'll get stuck on those little back-country roads." Sam didn't sound any happier. "We'll get off at a later exit."

Jessica flashed Tyler an embarrassed grin. She knew that *they'd* never argue about anything so stupid. *It's like Elizabeth and Sam are some old married couple already.* Jessica rolled her eyes. She was starting to seriously wonder if her idea to break them up was such a good one. After all, they were both being such pains, they deserved each other!

"I think we're lost." Elizabeth sounded worried. "Let's pull over and ask for directions."

"Look, Elizabeth," Sam was saying with barely

restrained politeness. "I don't have to ask anyone for directions. I'm perfectly capable of reading a map."

"I know you are, Sam." Jessica could tell that Elizabeth was gritting her teeth. "That's why it's so strange that we've been driving around in circles for the last twenty minutes."

Jessica sighed loudly. She had to admit that as much of a pain as her sister was being, Sam was even worse. Maybe it was Elizabeth's fault that they'd taken the wrong route, but Sam refused to stop and ask for directions. *What is it with men?* she thought irritably. It was almost as if by asking for help, Sam was afraid he'd be relinquishing his status as the alpha male.

"Uh, guys?" Tyler poked his head between the seats. "How about a compromise? If Sam doesn't find it in the next fifteen minutes, then we'll stop and *I'll* ask for directions."

"Thanks, Tyler," Jessica said quietly. Thank God *her* boyfriend could be reasonable. *Hmmm,* she thought. *My boyfriend.* She really couldn't call him that yet. But she liked the way it sounded. Who knew? Maybe by the time they arrived in Illinois, he would be her boyfriend!

"There's the sign!" Elizabeth pointed to an exit ramp for the San Diego Zoo.

"Finally." Jessica exhaled in relief. She shifted

uncomfortably on the seat. Her dress was sticking to her, and she had to use the bathroom.

"Sam! Will you watch the way you're parking?" Elizabeth's voice was starting to grate on Jessica's last nerve.

"What's wrong with the way I parked?" Sam got out of the Jeep and took a look. "Seems cool."

"You're, like, taking up two spaces," Elizabeth pointed out.

"Oh, who cares?" Jessica hopped out. "I want to *see* the monkeys." She took Tyler's arm. "*Not* spend all day cooped up in a car with them," she continued under her breath.

"Let's have lunch first," Elizabeth said. "Everyone in agreement?"

Three yeses followed, and they headed into the zoo's outdoor café.

"This is really nice," Jessica said as they sat down in wrought-iron chairs around a square table. She spread her pink linen napkin on her lap. Their table was shaded from the afternoon sun by a green-and-white-striped umbrella, and there was a small vase of pink roses in the center.

A waitress came over and handed them each menus. She signaled to a busboy to bring four waters to the table, then flipped open her order pad. As Jessica eyed the menu selections, she couldn't help noticing that the waitress was incredibly well built and wearing a skimpy halter. *Hey, as long as Tyler doesn't notice,* Jessica thought, smoothing down the front of her wrinkled sundress. She wasn't feeling her most attractive after driving all morning.

She smiled as Tyler barely acknowledged the waitress's presence. Then she frowned when she realized that Sam was ogling Ms. Big Boobs! *He is so crude!* Jessica fumed inwardly. She looked over at Elizabeth, prepared to offer a sympathetic smile, but Elizabeth was too engrossed in her menu to notice.

"Well," Elizabeth said brightly. "I'm up for the chicken salad and iced tea."

"The same for me," Jessica said quietly, studying Sam out of the corner of her eye as he placed his order. He didn't seem able to raise his eyes above the waitress's chest. *What is he, like twelve years old?* Jessica wondered. He was acting like he'd never seen a woman before.

Tyler ordered the same thing Sam did: a cheeseburger and fries and a Coke. In what seemed like a few minutes the waitress brought over a tray stacked with their orders. The burgers were probably nuked, Jessica realized. She watched Sam smile at Big Boobs as she set down his burger. His eyes were chest level again. What a jerk!

They were all so hungry and tired and cranky that lunch was a silent affair. Jessica was grateful when Big Boobs returned to clear away their plates. She figured Elizabeth would notice that Sam was checking the waitress out, but Elizabeth had her eyes closed, her face raised to the sun.

"So who wants to see the reptile house?" Sam looked around the table. "I'm into it."

I guess he wants to visit some relatives, Jessica thought.

Elizabeth opened her eyes and smiled. "Um, I'll go. I've always wanted to see a boa constrictor."

"Huh?" Jessica looked at her sister in surprise. Elizabeth had always hated snakes. Of course, that might have changed now that she was going out with one.

"Well, I'd rather check out the exotic birds," Tyler said over the rim of his soda glass. "Jess, does that work for you?"

"Sure." Jessica smiled at how thoughtful Tyler was. "I'd love to see some peacocks." She glanced at her watch. "So, what . . . we'll meet you guys back at the Jeep in an hour?"

"Sounds good," Elizabeth said, and they all stood up. "C'mon, Sam." She hooked her arm through his. "See you guys later."

"Jess," Tyler said as they strolled toward the bird sanctuary. "What's wrong?"

Jessica chewed on her lower lip as she eyed Sam and Elizabeth heading in the opposite direction. "I just have a bad feeling about Sam, Tyler. I don't trust him." She turned back to look at Tyler.

"Don't trust him with what?" Tyler sounded serious. "Are you afraid he'll take off or something?"

"No." Jessica rubbed her slender arms. In spite of the warmth of the day she felt unaccountably chilly. "I don't trust him with Elizabeth's heart." She felt foolish as soon as she said the words; she knew they sounded melodramatic. *But I can't help it—it's the way I feel,* she comforted herself.

Tyler draped his arm across her shoulders. "Listen, Jess, I think it's great that you're so protective of your sister. But I have to say, Sam seems like a good guy to me."

"Really?" Jessica was surprised. She moved closer to Tyler, enjoying the feel of his arm around her.

Tyler nodded. "Really. Not only that, but Elizabeth seems like she can take pretty good care of herself."

"That's true," Jessica said as they moved off toward the bird sanctuary. "But Elizabeth's kind of naive about guys like Sam. She—"

"Hey," Tyler interrupted, stopping them in their tracks. He moved them off the main path and onto a small gravel walkway that was sheltered by some overhanging willows. "Maybe you could stop stressing about Elizabeth for a second and pay some attention to me. I'm feeling like I might die . . ."

"Tyler!" Jessica gasped in alarm.

"If I don't kiss you," he finished softly, bending his head down to meet her lips.

Jessica nearly swooned. Tyler was right. It was time to stop stressing about Elizabeth. And time to start kissing Tyler . . .

"We should be there pretty soon," Elizabeth said with more confidence than she felt. She'd been driving steadily for the past four hours, and she needed a break in the worst way. The stop at the zoo had been great, but it seemed so long ago that it was almost like it had happened in another century.

"You said that ages ago," Jessica grumbled, half asleep, from the backseat.

"Wrong—I said that we were *halfway* there ages ago," Elizabeth snapped back. She was beginning to feel extremely cranky, her arms were getting sunburned, and she would have done anything for a cold drink. "We should have packed a cooler full of sodas." She sighed in irritation as she signaled a left turn.

"I *said* we should have," Sam agreed crankily. "But you guys insisted on loading up the Jeep with all sorts of useless stuff, so there wasn't any room."

Looks like I'm not the only one who needs a break, Elizabeth thought, glancing over at Sam, who was hunkered down in his seat and scowling at the map.

"So exactly how far do we have to go?" Tyler chimed in, rounding out the unhappy chorus.

"Actually, we're here," Elizabeth said as she pulled into the south entrance of the Grand Canyon.

"Whoa!" Sam got out of the Jeep and stood beside her. Even in the midst of the overcrowded parking lot it was impossible not to be blown away by the majestic beauty of the canyon. "Talk about awesome."

"It's incredible," Tyler exclaimed, staring out at the vast scenery.

"Wow!" Jessica shook her head in amazement as she looked around her. It was possible to see the crags and peaks of the distant rims from where they stood. "Too bad we didn't get here earlier and hike up to the top."

"You?" Sam hooted with laughter. "It's hardly your speed, Jessica. You can't hike the canyon in three-inch sling backs."

"Like you could really sprint up there anyway," Jessica shot back, giving him a dirty look. "Your idea of exercise is getting up to change the channels instead of using the remote."

"Hey, let it slide, Jess," Tyler said, laughing as he pulled her into his arms for an easy hug. "Sam's right about one thing. It is a pretty vicious hike—I doubt I'd be up for it."

"There's a free shuttle bus up to some of the overlooks on the south rim," Elizabeth said, glancing up from a glossy brochure. "Let's go that way—it only takes a few minutes, and we'll get some amazing views."

They all nodded, and Elizabeth led the way to the shuttle.

Once they were settled, Elizabeth rooted in her knapsack for her camera. "I can't believe I packed my camera at the bottom of my bag," she said mournfully as the shuttle began the climb toward the upper rims.

Sam shrugged. "So pick up a couple of post-cards in the gift shop."

"Sam!" Elizabeth swatted him with her hand. "That's hardly the same thing!"

"I can't believe we've arrived just in time for sunset!" Jessica enthused as the shuttle stopped at the top. "I mean, is that, like, too perfect?" She jumped out excitedly, and the rest of the crew followed.

"I've never seen anything like it," Elizabeth

murmured, reaching for Sam's hand, but Sam had already dashed ahead and was standing perilously close to the edge. She swallowed her disappointment and walked over to join him.

"Hey, Tyler, let's see if we can hear something hit the bottom," Sam yelled. "See if there are any pebbles." He sprinted away from the edge and started scrabbling in the dirt.

"Man, did you hear the way your voice echoed?" Tyler yelled back, much louder than necessary. "Intense!"

Elizabeth sighed. How could anybody's reaction—when faced with the astonishing beauty of the Grand Canyon—be to throw rocks and scream things? The sun was setting in a blaze of purple and scarlet. *It's like the perfect Kodak moment, and instead of holding my hand and staring at the view, Sam's running around like a little boy, trying to find the right-size pebbles. What's next? Frog jumping?*

"Looks like the canyon is really bringing out Sam's true colors," Jessica said as she wandered over to stand beside her at the edge.

"What's that supposed to mean?" Elizabeth gave her a sidelong look. She was already feeling sensitive about Sam's unromantic reaction, and she didn't need Jessica rubbing it in.

"Oh, I just mean the fact that he's rushing

around like a two-year-old on speed," Jessica replied, airily brushing a strand of hair out of her eyes.

"Like Tyler's acting so differently," Elizabeth pointed out. She gestured toward where Tyler was running around, grabbing various pebbles to throw over the edge.

"That's just Sam's bad influence," Jessica replied.

"Why are you so down on Sam?" Elizabeth snapped. "You just won't even give him a chance, Jess. He's way more thoughtful and way more mature than you know. I mean, he's been on his own without benefit of his family's support for a while now. Don't you think that takes a special kind of maturity?"

"Hey, Tyler," Sam called out as he ran by. "How loud a splat do you think someone makes when they fall over the edge?"

Jessica smirked at Elizabeth. "You were saying?"

Elizabeth sighed.

Chapter Eight

"Okay, I'm stopping at the next place we come to," Sam announced as they sped down the highway in search of a place to stay the night. "I mean it, guys, I don't care if it's the Bates motel. Hey, have you guys seen the movie *Psycho*? It's this Hitchcock flick, and this creepy guy runs this hotel, and—"

"Can you shut up, please?" Jessica snapped. "I don't need to think of getting stabbed to death in the shower at some fleabag hotel, Sam."

"Guys, c'mon," Tyler said a bit wearily. "There should be a rest stop somewhere around here." He peered out the window at the deepening sky. "We can ask there."

Elizabeth tapped Sam's arm. "Hey, slow down. I think I see a sign up ahead for a B and B."

Sam squinted to read the sign. "Red River

Ranch B and B, exit twelve, five miles." He shrugged. "It sounds a little cheesy, but what the hell. Probably better than the Bates."

"Stop saying that," Jessica complained from the backseat. "You'll give me nightmares."

Sam was about to retort when Elizabeth shot him a look. He rolled his eyes and turned his attention back to the road.

"Oh my gosh," Elizabeth exclaimed as they pulled into the B and B's driveway. "It looks like something out of a movie!"

"It does, kind of," Sam agreed as he parked the Jeep. He hopped out and stretched his legs. Elizabeth, Tyler, and Jessica all did the same.

"Kind of like a retro ghost town," Jessica said, looking at the tumbleweeds blowing around the door.

Tyler pointed toward the steer horns that served as door handles. "I'd say more like *nouveau western*."

"Well, whatever it looks like, it's cheap," Sam said, nodding at the sign. "Twenty-five bucks a night says it's the perfect place. I'm going inside to see if they have any vacancies."

After spending all day in a car with Jessica, he was grateful for the break, even if it was only for five minutes. *And she's not the only one I need a break from,* Sam thought glumly as he pulled open the door to the B and B. Having Elizabeth play "backseat" driver hadn't been the most relaxing experience either. He felt like she'd been at him all day—if she wasn't bothering him about his parking skills, she was screaming that he was about to miss an exit.

"Hey, anyone around?" he called as he approached the reception desk and rang the bell.

"Just a sec," a musical voice said. "I'll be right out."

Sam drummed his fingers impatiently on the desk as he waited for the woman to come out. He looked around the lobby, barely registering the brass spittoons that were dotted around; he was too preoccupied with thoughts of Elizabeth.

Why did she have to be so clingy today? he wondered. It was almost as if driving to his cousin's wedding made Elizabeth feel that they were an old married couple. *She sounded like my mother. Worse, she sounded like my wife!*

"Can I help you?"

Sam turned around. *Whoa!* The reception clerk smiled at him pleasantly. *She looks like she could have modeled for Barbie!*

Sam brought his eyes up to her face and flashed her his brightest smile. "I'm sure that you'll be able to help me." He couldn't help moving into flirting mode. A sweet-faced stranger who

137

wouldn't nag him was exactly what he needed at the moment! "I need a bedroom," he said slowly, overenunciating the word *bedroom*.

"Single, I hope?" she asked, a shy smile tugging at her pretty mouth.

Well, she's sure picking up on the vibe, Sam thought with a grin. He had an uncomfortable prickling in the back of his mind, but he pushed it firmly aside. *What's wrong with a little flirting?* he asked himself. *It's not like I'm proposing or anything, and I deserve a little fun after the way Elizabeth nagged me all day!*

"And what if I said yes?" He leaned against the reception desk, his heart beating double time. *What am I doing?* Sam asked himself. He wasn't really interested in this girl, and even if he was, he wouldn't want to do anything with her. Sam would agree with Jessica that he deserved to be called a lot of names, but *sleaze* wasn't one of them. And playing around on Elizabeth definitely qualified as sleazy.

"Hmmm," the girl murmured. "So, I guess that means you're free to take me out for a drink or something tonight—"

"Sam!"

He gulped and turned around. He found himself staring straight into Jessica's eyes. *Thank God she isn't Elizabeth!* "Uh, h-hey, Jess . . . ," he stammered.

138

What the clerk had said did sound sort of bad.

"I just came in to say that Tyler and I wanted two *single* beds in our room," Jessica said, her eyes snapping back and forth between Sam and the clerk. "But I wouldn't want to interrupt you!" She stormed out of the tiny lobby, slamming the door behind her.

Busted, Sam thought, groaning. *Does Jess have radar or something?* "Hey, I, uh, actually need a *double* room for myself," he told the clerk shamefacedly. He tried to give her a smile, but it came out kind of lopsided. "And you heard the blonde," he added.

"No problem, sweetie," she said, breaking into a sly grin. "Too bad you're taken. But you're not married, are ya?"

He shook his head. He most certainly was not! "Well, uh, see you around."

He opened the door cautiously, half expecting Elizabeth to be standing outside, demanding an explanation.

"Phew." Sam breathed a sigh of relief when he saw that the coast was clear. Elizabeth was helping Tyler unload the Jeep, and Jessica was nowhere in sight.

I guess Jessica kept her mouth shut for once, Sam realized. He shoved his hands in his pockets and started trudging toward the car. *Hey, wait a minute*. He stopped in his tracks. *What am I stressing for? I talked to a girl—so what? Get a grip, dude.* He shook his head in disgust. *Stop acting like you were just caught between the sheets, and stop worrying about Jessica. You've got nothing to feel bad about,* he reassured himself as he approached Elizabeth and Tyler.

But he couldn't help wondering why, if that was true, that he couldn't bring himself to meet his girlfriend's eyes or why he had such a sinking feeling in his stomach.

"This must be it, guys," Elizabeth said, her hand on the saloon doors. "There's nowhere else around, right?" The B and B's clerk, who Jessica had been very rude to for some odd reason, had told them the saloon was the only place open for miles around. *It looks like a hoot,* Elizabeth thought, peering through the slotted doors.

"Let's go in—I'm starving," Jessica said behind her. "I'm really in the mood for a good spinach salad."

"Uh, something tells me that they don't serve anything like that here, Jess," Elizabeth pointed out as they walked into the tavern. "A side of beef, maybe."

The room had more pool tables than dining tables, one wall was dominated by a giant dartboard, and there was sawdust on the floor.

Sam seemed happy as he led the way over to a table. "This looks pretty cool."

"Yeah," Tyler agreed with a smile. "It certainly has atmosphere."

"Yeah, what kind is another matter," Jessica muttered under her breath.

"I think it's fun." Elizabeth grinned as she looked up at the blackboard that served as a menu. "Hmmm." She quickly scanned the choices. "What'll it be, guys? Ribs, ribs, or ribs?"

"I guess I'll have the ribs," Jessica said.

"I'm going to go for the *free* ribs," Sam announced. He leaned back and crossed his arms in front of his chest.

"Free ribs?" Tyler raised his eyebrows. "How're you planning that one, buddy?"

Sam grinned. "I'm gonna win them. I'm going to win them for all of us." He gestured toward the giant dartboard on the wall. Elizabeth noticed a sign above it, proclaiming that whoever beat the house record would win all the ribs they could eat.

"Uh, Sam, I'm kind of hungry," Elizabeth said. "Maybe we should just order and you can play darts after dinner."

Sam frowned. "Are you kidding? It's the best idea I've had all day." He stood up and sauntered over to the bar, where he picked up a handful of darts.

141

"Listen, Lizzie," Jessica said, her irritation evident. "I really want to eat and get back to the hotel. Do we really have to sit around and watch your boyfriend lose at darts?"

"Hey, let him throw a couple," Tyler said reasonably. "Can't hurt, and maybe we'll win a free dinner."

"Just so you know, hon," a waitress called to Sam as she set water glasses on their table. "Nobody's *ever* beaten the house record."

"Okay, waiting around for Sam to win is a really beat idea," Jessica exclaimed, taking a sip of her water.

Sam threw his first dart.

"Wow, that was perfect!" Tyler whistled. Sam landed his first bull's-eye with his first throw.

"Go, Sam!" Elizabeth clapped. She noticed that several of the guys playing pool had stopped to watch Sam. She had to admit that he was worth watching. Sam looked incredibly sexy as he frowned in concentration, the muscles of his biceps bunched up under his T-shirt as he let loose with the second dart, which landed smack in the center of the board.

"This one's for you, Liz," Sam called over his shoulder as he threw another one.

"Looks like your friend might just beat the record," the waitress said in astonishment as she

142

returned with a round of iced teas. "Why don't you all tell me how you like your ribs?" She whipped a pencil out from behind her ear.

"Make mine with extra barbecue sauce," Sam said, winking at Elizabeth. There were so many darts collected in the center of the board that it didn't look like there was room for any more.

"Make mine rare," Tyler said. "Hey, Sam, buy you a beer?" He grinned. "I mean, it's the least I can do."

"Sure," Sam said. He then shook hands with all the guys who'd been playing pool. He held court, sharing his tips for perfect aims. By the time he slid onto the bench next to Elizabeth, she took in his wild hair, the slightly sweaty masculinity of him, and felt her heart about to burst.

"Miss me while I was gone?" He kissed her cheek.

"You know it," Elizabeth whispered, kissing him back. "Thanks for winning dinner," she said softly as the waitress placed several platters of ribs and fixings in front of them.

"Nothing to it," Sam said with a satisfied grin. He bit into a rib. "I have a lot of hidden talents that you don't know about."

I'll bet, Elizabeth thought as she wiped a smear of barbecue sauce off his cheek. She wondered how often Sam had played darts. She knew that he didn't accept any financial support from his parents. Did he use his skills at dart playing to help support himself? He'd mentioned that the money his grandparents had left him barely covered his tuition and rent. He had to do something to make a little extra to live on.

Once Elizabeth would have been shocked at that kind of thing, but right now all she could be was impressed at Sam's survival skills. *Sam's really had to deal with a lot,* she thought, a lump forming in her throat.

"Dude, these are really excellent," Tyler exclaimed, munching appreciatively. "I really owe you."

"Yeah?" Sam took a swig of his beer. "How about you and me shoot a couple of rounds of pool afterward?"

"Sounds cool." Tyler reached for some more ribs. "Of course, it may take me a while to finish, but sure, I'd love to sink a few balls."

"Are you sure you want to, Tyler?" Jessica asked, a distinct edge to her voice. "I mean, we haven't had a chance to be alone together all day."

Sam wiped his fingers on a red-and-white-checked napkin. "Chill, Jess. You two didn't even get a double bed, so what's the rush?"

Jessica's cheeks flamed, and she stared at Sam in disbelief. "You are so crude!"

Uh-oh, time for a little damage control, Elizabeth

thought. She threw her napkin on the table and stood up hastily. "C'mon, Jess, we've all had a long day. How about we let the guys shoot some pool and we go on a walk?"

Jessica sighed. "All right." She stood up, but she didn't look pleased.

"Hey, see you guys back at the hotel." Elizabeth smiled and reached for her cardigan, glad that she'd been able to avert a disaster. But she couldn't get over what Sam had said.

Well, imagine that. She shook her head in wonder as she led the way to the door. *Jessica's sleeping on a single bed, and I'm sharing one with Sam. Who would've thought?*

"It sure is a gorgeous night," Jessica said, gazing up at the sky.

Somehow the stars seemed extra twinkly out here near the desert. It was so romantic that she couldn't help wishing she was with Tyler instead of her sister. *But I guess Tyler would rather hang out in a smoky restaurant and shoot pool with that sleazy slacker than go for a walk in the moonlight with me,* Jessica thought bitterly.

Oh, well, I better make the best of it, she told herself, trying to shake off her sour mood. She knew that Tyler felt he couldn't say no to Sam; after all, the guy had just bought them all dinner.

And even though she was glad to be alone with her sister for a while, still . . . "Hey, look," Jessica exclaimed. "Do you think that's a shooting star? That's so cool!"

"It's amazing," Elizabeth agreed, but she didn't seem to be especially moved. "Look, Jess, I don't want to talk about the stars. I want to know what Sam was referring to back there in the restaurant."

"What Sam was referring to?" Jessica mimicked Elizabeth's voice sarcastically. "Don't you mean to say what your *crude boyfriend* blurted out?"

"Let's not argue, Jess," Elizabeth snapped. "Please?" She looked at her sister with a pleading expression on her face. "Look, I can see why what he said bothered you, and it wasn't exactly delicate. But I guess Sam's just tired. He wasn't thinking—that's all."

"Like he ever thinks," Jessica said bitterly.

"Oh, come on, Jess. Let's talk about what really matters." Elizabeth stopped walking and studied Jessica's face in the moonlight. "What's going on between you and Tyler?"

Jessica wasn't about to let Sam off that easily, but she did want to talk to Elizabeth about her own guy. "Just so you know, I haven't forgiven Sam," she stated, bending to pick a wildflower that was growing by the side of the road. "But I'll

146

let it go this time because you're right—I'd rather talk about Tyler. Oh, Lizzie, isn't he amazing?"

"He certainly seems pretty great." Elizabeth smiled.

"*Pretty* great?" Jessica practically shrieked. "What do you mean, *pretty* great? He's perfect! I mean, he's gorgeous, sensitive, kind, gorgeous—"

"Okay." Elizabeth laughed. "I get the picture, and I have to say I can see why you're so crazy about him. So why the separate beds?"

"Well, that doesn't sound like the Elizabeth we all know and love," Jessica said, amused. "I mean, you're arguing *against* separate beds? C'mon, Liz, you can tell me the truth. Did Sam slip a little something in your iced tea?"

"I wish," Elizabeth murmured. "No, really, Jessica, what's going on?"

Did Elizabeth just say that she wished Sam had slipped something in her iced tea? Jessica shook her head as if she was trying to clear it. *I must be hearing things.* "I just want to take things slowly, that's all," she explained. "There's no need to rush. Tyler and I have all summer to get to know each other."

"Mmmm, that's exactly what Sam says," Elizabeth said distractedly.

"Huh?" Jessica frowned. "You and Sam have been talking about me and Tyler?"

"No, silly." Elizabeth laughed. "I mean, that's what Sam says about the two of us. I'm ready to sleep with him, Jess, but he wants to take things slowly. He wants to wait a while."

Okay, now I know I'm hearing things. "You know what, Elizabeth? I think Sam slipped something in *my* iced tea. I swear I just heard you say that you wanted to have sex with Sam!"

"I did," Elizabeth said simply.

"Omigod!" Jessica's mouth hung open. *She can't lose her virginity to that five-timing cheat! How can I talk her out of it?* "Are you sure you want to do this, Lizzie?" she asked in as gentle a voice as she could manage. "I mean, it's, like, a *huge* step—once you take it, there's no going back. Besides, you and Sam have only been an official couple for a little while. Don't you think it's too soon?"

"So maybe we've only been dating for a little while, but we've been living together for almost a year." Elizabeth giggled. "I mean, we *really* know each other. At least I think we do. I have to say, Sam's more like you. He thinks we should wait."

"*Sam* thinks you should wait?" Jessica gaped at her sister. *That* was almost as shocking as Elizabeth wanting to have sex. *This can't be true—he's up to something. What kind of guy turns down a beautiful virgin?*

"Yup, he wants to wait. I was a little bit disappointed at first, but now I can see how romantic he's being."

"Yeah, sure, he's being really romantic," Jessica said. She put a hand to her head; it was spinning so fast that she didn't think she could stand up anymore. She was sure that Sam was playing some kind of weird game, but she didn't know what.

Tyler. I need to talk to Tyler about this, Jessica realized. Tyler was a guy, and more than that, he strangely seemed to have some idea of how the Burgess mind worked. Tyler would be able to explain what Sam was doing.

Plus he can help me plan how to kill Sam, Jessica thought grimly as she and Elizabeth headed back to the motel.

Well, okay, maybe I won't kill Sam, she decided, quickening her pace. *Maybe I'll just torture him for a little bit, but one thing's for sure—no way am I going to let him break my sister's heart!*

Chapter Nine

Should I put on that black lace nightgown? Elizabeth wondered as she sat on the bed and brushed her hair. She looked down at the over-sized baseball jersey she was wearing. The sleep shirt was definitely more her style, or it used to be anyway. But she hadn't been able to get the night-gown out of her mind ever since she'd seen it while shopping with Nina. Elizabeth had gone back by herself and bought it, and even though she hadn't worn the nightgown yet, she was glad that she'd stashed it in her suitcase.

What would Sam think if he came out of the shower and saw me in it? She couldn't help pictur-ing the scene. Would he sweep her into his arms? Would he forget the fact that he thought they should wait? Would they finally make love?

Elizabeth glanced at the bathroom door. She

could hear Sam warbling off-key above the rushing water of the shower. What would happen if she didn't put on the nightgown? What would happen if she went in the bathroom instead? She could join him in the shower, and they could . . .

She slowly stood up, her heart pounding wildly, and walked toward the bathroom door. *I can't believe I'm going to do this,* she thought nervously, reaching for the doorknob. Before she could change her mind, she pulled open the door.

"What's up—you want to brush your teeth?" Sam grinned at her. He was standing in front of the mirror with a towel wrapped around his waist. "No prob—I'll be out in a second."

"It's okay; you don't have to hurry," Elizabeth said, swallowing her disappointment. She couldn't believe that now that she'd gotten up the courage to be really adventurous, she was being foiled at every turn.

"You look really cute in that baseball shirt," Sam said as he brushed past her. "Kind of like a little girl in her father's clothes."

Great, Elizabeth thought with a grimace. *That sounds really sexy.* She sighed as she reached for the toothpaste. *Oh, well, so we won't be getting hot and heavy tonight. So what? We'll have a really romantic time just holding each other. . . .*

"Hey, Elizabeth," Sam called out.

She peered through the ajar bathroom door. Sam, who'd exchanged the towel for sexy boxer shorts, was flopped crosswise on the bed, pointing the remote control at the television.

It's like it's his third hand or something, Elizabeth thought.

"Guess what?" He sounded as excited as a little puppy. "They've got Nick at Nite here! Do you know what that means?"

"Old sitcoms?" Elizabeth guessed. She walked toward the bed. That would be fun, she decided. They'd snuggle up on the bed, maybe share some popcorn—if the vending machine in the hall had any. Elizabeth loved TV shows from the sixties and seventies, and right now, snuggling under the covers and watching one with Sam sounded really romantic.

She plopped down on the bed and kissed Sam on the cheek. How many boyfriends would be that romantic? Sam was so sensitive. Every time she worried about his reaction to her bombshell about "being ready," she had to keep in mind that he was a really thoughtful person. He simply wanted to make sure she was ready, that she wasn't simply announcing she was ready just because she fancied herself in love.

"What's on?" she asked, curling up beside him. *"The Partridge Family? That Girl? Bewitched?"*

"Are you kidding?" Sam looked at her as if she were crazy. "Much better than that! Man, they have classic 'toons on this station! The lost Rocky and Bullwinkle episodes are on next!"

"Great," Elizabeth said dully. "I really need to catch up on those." She glanced briefly at the television, where Natasha and Boris Badenov were dancing the tango. *How come Natasha knows how to seduce a man?* Elizabeth wondered glumly.

"I know—me too!" Sam was transfixed by the screen. "You know, this is really turning out to be some trip!"

It sure is, Elizabeth thought, sighing as she burrowed under the covers. She pulled the pillow over her head. They had to be up early in the morning, and there was no way she was going to be able to sleep with Natasha and Boris jabbering at each other all night.

"You've just got the best shoulders," Jessica said as she watched Tyler strip off his shirt. She was sitting up in bed with her knees hugged to her chest. *Maybe I made the wrong decision,* she thought wistfully as Tyler walked across the room to his own bed. *Maybe we should have just gotten a double bed.* After all, there was no law that said sharing the same bed meant they would automatically end up sleeping with each other.

153

Yeah, right, Jessica thought with a smirk. *Like I could keep my hands off a body like that!*

"Hey, what's with the long face?" Tyler grinned at her as he plopped down on his back. "You miss me over here?"

"You bet," Jessica said with a sigh. "But . . . I just think we should take things slow for a while."

"I know, sweetheart," he said. "No pressure. You call the shots, Jess. I mean, hey, it doesn't take a rocket scientist to figure out that I'd love to be sharing that bed with you, but it's really up to you."

"You're too good to be true," Jessica said, playing with the fringe on her blanket. "I just don't want to rush things. I like you too much for that, you know?"

He smiled. "Ditto for me, beautiful. But as long as you trust me to scoot back over here whenever you say, how about I come over there and give you a back rub?"

"Sounds heavenly." Jessica flopped over on her stomach, glancing at Tyler as he moved to the foot of her bed and sat down at her feet. "Don't be too hard."

"How's this?" He kneaded her delicate shoulders gently, his strong hands turning her knotted muscles into butter.

"Mmmm, perfect." Jessica sighed in contentment. "Tyler? Can I ask you something?"

"Shoot," he said, his hands caressing her lower back.

"You said that it was up to me. I mean, that I could put on the brakes."

He removed his hands. "Do you want me to stop?"

"Yeah, like in about twenty hours," she replied, chuckling. "I'm getting at something else." Jessica turned her head slightly so she could see Tyler's face. "I just have this really bad feeling about Sam. . . ." She trailed off, unsure of how to continue.

"You mean, you think he won't respect Elizabeth if *she* wants to put on the brakes?" Tyler asked. "I've got to tell you that isn't the vibe I get from him, Jess."

"No, I don't mean that at all—more the opposite." Jessica frowned. "Elizabeth told me that she would sleep with Sam, but that *he* thinks they should wait. Now, you tell me, what kind of guy turns down a girl who looks like Elizabeth?" She turned over on her stomach and looked at Tyler with a confused expression on her face.

"That's, like, a little weird," Tyler admitted. "Considering that she looks exactly like you, and I couldn't turn you down!" He laughed, then turned serious again. "Unless—" He paused for a second, tilting his head. "Unless Elizabeth is a virgin."

Jessica nodded. "She is. You think that has something to do with it?"

"Probably a lot." Tyler leaned back against the pillows. "Either Sam is way in love with Elizabeth and he's nervous about taking her virginity—"

"Scratch that," Jessica interrupted, propping herself up on one elbow. "He's hardly Mr. Sensitive. I can't see him getting that nervous or caring that much."

"Well, the other thing I can think of is that he's worried that if he takes her virginity, he'll be obligated to her in some way. Maybe he's really into her, but he doesn't want to stick around forever. Maybe he doesn't want her getting too clingy."

"That's got to be it!" Jessica exclaimed, hitting the blanket with her fist. "Oh, man, he is so low! I can't stand the thought of Elizabeth being with him!"

"Hey, Jess, chill a little, okay?" Tyler said mildly. "Elizabeth's a big girl. I see the way Sam looks at her—"

"When he's not checking out busty waitresses," Jessica fumed.

"Yeah, okay, so he's a *guy*." Tyler shrugged. "Seriously, Jess, anyone can see that Sam really cares about Elizabeth. He's probably just a little scared—that's all."

"Trust me, Tyler," Jessica said stubbornly. "I

156

know I'm right on this one. I've got to tell Elizabeth what his game is."

"Look," Tyler said patiently. "Even if you're right and Sam really is a bad guy, telling Elizabeth won't do any good. That's something she has to find out for herself." He twisted a lock of her hair around his fingers. "You know, Jess, I get the feeling that Elizabeth's tried to warn you before, that there have been plenty of situations when you've made the wrong choice. Am I right?"

Jessica smiled sheepishly. "Yeah, I guess."

"And did her telling you do any good?"

"No," Jessica admitted. "Okay, I get the message. So, anything else you want to tell me?"

"Nothing else I want to *tell* you," Tyler drawled. "But as long as we're on the subject of what men and women do together . . ." He gave a sexy smile as he lowered his mouth on hers.

Chapter Ten

"Ugh." Elizabeth grimaced as she rubbed her lower back. "Did anyone else feel like their mattress was stuffed with corncobs?"

"Try pebbles," Jessica grumbled, slipping on a pair of oversized sunglasses to cover her makeup-free eyes.

"What do you mean, 'pebbles'?" Tyler groaned. "Pebbles are little, they're cute—try *boulders*."

"My back isn't that bad, but I'm starving," Sam added to the chorus. "Where are we going to eat?"

"Beats me." Elizabeth shrugged. They'd overslept breakfast at the hotel, and it didn't seem like there was anyplace else around. "I guess we'll have to settle for whatever they're selling at the nearest gas station."

"Breakfast of champions," Jessica said sourly.

"But hey, it should be right up your alley, Burgess. I mean, you *like* microwave nachos."

Elizabeth gave Jessica a look of extreme irritation.

Sam shrugged. "It's too bad that you aren't into them, Jess, because we probably won't be stopping for lunch for a while."

Elizabeth blinked in surprise. Sam usually rose to Jessica's bait, but this time his answer had been exceptionally mild.

"Why don't we head over to the gas station now?" Tyler suggested. "We need to fuel up anyway."

"You're right," Elizabeth said as she slid behind the wheel. Her whole body felt sore, and she wasn't looking forward to being stuck in the Jeep all day.

As she drove onto the road, Elizabeth was grateful that her cranky passengers were too tired to complain or argue.

"Whoa!" Sam exclaimed as they pulled into the gas station. "These prices are, like, way out of line!"

Elizabeth blinked in surprise. "They do seem a little high."

"I'm going to get us some food," Tyler said, jumping out of the car.

"Yeah, grab me two of whatever you're getting," Sam called after him.

"I guess we should fill up the tank," Elizabeth said. "There aren't exactly a lot of places to comparison shop here."

Sam looked at her. "With prices like this, we might need to rethink our route."

"What do you mean?" Jessica asked.

"I mean that all those scenic little detours that you and Elizabeth picked out are going to eat up gas like it's going out of style."

"But Sam," Elizabeth protested, her heart sinking. "Those detours make sense because we're still staying on the major highways. I'm really counting on seeing Santa Fe."

"Yeah, so am I," Jessica insisted. "Santa Fe is, like, way high on my list, and I don't feel like cutting it out just because you've decided that it doesn't fit in our budget."

Really? Elizabeth raised her eyebrows. That was weird. She'd practically had to twist Jessica's arm to get her to agree to Santa Fe. *She's just spoiling for a fight,* Elizabeth realized. She only hoped that it wouldn't be too bad. She was sick of reffing. But from the look on Jessica's face it seemed like she was on the warpath, and Sam didn't look too happy either.

"And anyway," Jessica continued, "if you're worried about the prices, why don't you pay? You're the only one here with rich parents."

"Jessica!" Elizabeth said, shocked. She couldn't believe that Jessica had delivered such a low blow. She knew as well as Elizabeth that Sam didn't take

160

any money from his parents. She glanced uneasily at Sam; she wasn't surprised to see that he was turning bright red with anger.

"In fact," Jessica snapped, "I don't see why Tyler should contribute at all."

"You're way out of line," Sam fumed.

"Jess." Elizabeth laid a placating hand on her sister's arm. "The deal was that Tyler pays all gas and tolls to Illinois."

"Well, if Sam gets to rethink the route, I get to rethink the deal," Jessica said.

Elizabeth struggled to keep her voice even. "You're both acting like third graders! Do you think you could try and be a little more reasonable?"

"I *am* being reasonable," Jessica flared. "He's getting to use our Jeep as free transportation to Boston!" She jerked her thumb at Sam. "So why shouldn't *he* pay for the gas?"

"I'm getting to use the Jeep for free too," Tyler pointed out as he walked up behind them. He carried several wrapped sandwiches. "And besides, a deal is a deal. I said I'd pay to Illinois, and I'm paying. End of discussion." He passed out the sandwiches. "So what is the problem here?"

The problem is that Sam and Jessica both woke up on the wrong side of their corncob-stuffed mattresses, Elizabeth thought, flashing Tyler a look of gratitude.

161

"Let's just get a move on, okay?" She smiled at the group, but Tyler was the only one who smiled back. "We're all in pretty crappy moods. I'm sure we'll feel better once we hit the road."

"I'm sure we'll feel better once we hit someplace decent for *lunch*," Jessica said, dumping her sausage-and-egg sandwich in the trash.

"Whatever," Elizabeth said, peering at her own sandwich. Her stomach turned at the sight of the rubbery-looking eggs. She tossed it in the trash too and climbed into the Jeep. "Let's drive."

Things have to get better, she told herself as she reversed out of the station. *I mean, they couldn't possibly get worse, could they?*

She floored the gas and hit the highway at top speed.

"Damn, and they say the camera never lies." Sam shook his head in amazement as he climbed out of the Jeep and looked around him. "I mean, this is way, way more beautiful than any picture I've seen. Look at the color of those!" He swept his hand toward the dunes on the horizon, which were a constantly shifting kaleidoscope of dusty pink and caramel. "Now I get why they call it the Painted Desert."

"It is gorgeous," Elizabeth said quietly as she stood beside him.

Sam stared at the panoramic view laid out before him. He was truly awestruck. *Or maybe I'm just so thrilled to get out of the Jeep that anything would look good,* he thought. Being cooped up with Jessica all day was starting to wear on him. Luckily she and Tyler had fallen asleep about a hundred miles back, and the ride had been blissfully silent.

"C'mon." Elizabeth grabbed his hand. "Let's spread out the picnic."

Sam smiled at her. Sometimes she was so sweet and thoughtful that it truly amazed him. She'd spotted an advertisement for a gourmet market as they'd sped along the highway, and while Tyler and Jessica napped, she'd taken a detour and bought them all a fabulous picnic lunch. Elizabeth had insisted that they all deserved it after the gas-station breakfast, and she'd also insisted on paying for it herself.

"Right here should be perfect." She lifted the basket out of the Jeep and laid a bright red-and-white-checked cloth down on the sand.

"This stuff looks great," Sam said as he watched her unwrap containers of fried chicken and brownies. "And so do you," he couldn't resist adding. Elizabeth was always pretty, but today she seemed especially gorgeous in a pair of white shorts and a red halter that showed off her slim curves to perfection.

"Thanks." Elizabeth blew him a kiss. "Hey, you want to wake the others up?"

Not really. The smile faded from Sam's face. "To tell the truth, I'd rather just let them sleep and have you all to myself."

"Too late," Elizabeth said regretfully. "Looks like they smelled the fried chicken." She pointed toward the Jeep. Tyler and Jessica emerged, blinking at the sunlight and looking dazed.

"That smells fab." Jessica sniffed appreciatively as they came over. "This is a mirage, right?" She sank down on the sand and picked up a piece of fried chicken. "I mean, you're going to pinch me and I'll find out that we never left that gross gas station, right?"

"Tastes pretty good for a mirage," Tyler commented as he plucked a brownie and took a bite.

"This was all Elizabeth's idea," Sam said. He sat down beside her and reached for the container of potato salad. "This really is great."

"This place is totally awesome." Tyler reached down and grabbed a handful of sand. He watched transfixed as the red dust trickled through his fingers. "Does anyone know how the sand got to be this color?"

"What about the rocks?" Jessica waved her hand at the rock formations that dotted the landscape, each one striped in stunning colors.

164

Elizabeth took a swig of her lemonade. "It's a mixture of volcanic ash and silica that makes the color."

"That's right!" Tyler exclaimed.

"How'd you know that?" Sam was impressed. Sometimes he forgot just how smart Elizabeth was.

Face it, dude, you never forget how special this chick is. He brushed back a lock of Elizabeth's hair that was blowing in the wind. *It's just that it's hard to think about that when she gets all nagging and needy.*

Still, he had to admit that she was hardly nagging now. In fact, she hadn't said a word about his driving or parking all day. *Why can't Elizabeth always act like this?* He sighed. Right now things seemed so uncomplicated. It felt incredible to be out in the middle of nowhere surrounded by such amazing beauty with Elizabeth at his side.

"So how long before we have to hit the road?" Tyler asked, glancing at his watch.

"We should leave soon if we want to get to Santa Fe before dinner," Elizabeth said regretfully.

"Really?" Jessica seemed disappointed. "The desert looks so cool, I kind of wanted to explore for a while."

"You know there are rattlesnakes here, Jessica," Sam said mischievously.

165

"Whaa?" Jessica jumped about ten feet in the air.

"Just kidding." Sam grinned. "There aren't any snakes here. At least I don't think there are. Hey, since we all seem to be so hot on the desert, why don't we camp out tonight? There are some great places around Santa Fe we can check out. C'mon . . ." He squeezed Elizabeth's hand; she was looking extremely unconvinced. "Just imagine sleeping under the stars. It will be really romantic."

"Well, I think it's a great idea," Tyler said. "The sand can't be worse than the mattresses we had last night!"

"That's for sure," Jessica said rubbing her lower back.

Sam nodded. "And we can save money too. Okay with you, Elizabeth?"

"Sure." Elizabeth smiled. "As long as there aren't any snakes."

"If there are, I'll protect you," Sam whispered in her ear. He was glad that she'd agreed to sleep out because all of a sudden there was nothing he'd rather do than spend the night under the stars with Elizabeth in his arms.

"This place is so wild, maybe I should transfer here next year," Jessica exclaimed as she and Tyler wandered in and out of the funky arts-and-crafts stores in downtown Santa Fe.

"Your parents would probably freak," Tyler said, examining a hand-tooled leather belt. "Sweet Valley U is pretty highly rated. I bet they wouldn't be into you switching schools."

More like I would freak, Jessica thought as she watched Tyler move around the store. She'd only known him for a week, but she was already having a hard time imagining life without him. They had an incredible connection—one Jessica hadn't had with a guy in a long, long time. It was almost as if they could read each other's minds. If she started a sentence, he finished it. Not only that, but he was also completely sophisticated and mature, and even though Jessica hadn't seen any of his work, she was sure that he was incredibly talented.

And on top of everything else he's completely gorgeous! Jessica couldn't help but notice the admiring glances that Tyler was attracting as he moved through the store. *Back off, honey, he's mine!* she felt like growling to a particularly cute redhead. The redhead looked like she was itching to get to know Tyler better, and Jessica had no intention of letting that happen. She grabbed Tyler firmly by the elbow and led him outside onto the pavement.

Tyler looked at her in surprise. "Didn't you want to check out the earrings in there? I thought you were interested in some turquoise ones."

"Oh, I just wanted to get outside in the sunshine,"

Jessica replied airily. But she couldn't help being impressed by Tyler's thoughtfulness. Most guys had an allergy to shopping, but Tyler was willing to help her look for earrings. Very cool.

"Do you mind if we check out some of the galleries?" Tyler asked. "There are quite a few really famous ones around here."

"Sure, I'd love to visit some galleries," Jessica agreed enthusiastically. *Maybe we'll come live here after we're married,* she thought dreamily. *Tyler can spend all day painting, and maybe I'll handle his press or something.*

"So what do you think of this?" Tyler asked as they walked into an exhibit and stopped in front of a large, colorful painting.

"Hmmm." Jessica cocked her head. She'd learned a lot about painting in her art-history classes, but she certainly didn't know as much as Tyler, and she didn't want to make a fool of herself in front of him.

"I guess I'd have to say that figuratively it reminds me of Kandinsky." Jessica frowned as she studied the painting more closely. "But this artist uses a bolder palette," she said.

"Jessica, you're amazing!" Tyler laughed. "I certainly didn't know that much after a couple of art-history classes. But I was really more interested in how the painting affected you personally. Do you like it?"

"Not really," Jessica admitted. "I'm more into the impressionist thing."

"I feel the same way." Tyler nodded. "In fact, that's the style I'd like to paint you in."

"Really?" Jessica glowed. She was thrilled that he agreed with her and even happier that he was still interested in painting her.

"Really." Tyler smiled. "Listen, I want to go and ask the assistant how to get to the Payson gallery. I know it's around here somewhere, and they've got the biggest collection of early-twentieth-century European art in the country. I'll be right back." He kissed her cheek and walked over to the guy seated at the desk.

Jessica wandered over to the next painting. This one was even more abstract. Bright slashes of red and green paint covered the canvas.

"Kind of looks like a busted traffic light, doesn't it?"

Jessica turned to see a cute guy in his midtwenties smiling at her. He wasn't gorgeous and sophisticated like Tyler, but he had kind of a cowboy quality that was ultra-appealing.

"You're right." She laughed, turning back to the painting. "It does look like a broken traffic light."

"I bet you've stopped traffic pretty often yourself." The guy's smile deepened, revealing twin dimples.

Flirt alert! Jessica wondered if she should tell him that she was heavily involved. She looked over her shoulder to where Tyler was busily chatting with the assistant. *But it's not like this is going to lead to anything, and it doesn't hurt to keep the skills intact.*

"Depends on who's behind the wheel," Jessica said slowly.

"Well, if I were the one driving, there'd be, like, a seven-car pileup." The guy smiled.

Not bad. Jessica felt the familiar tingle that came from tangling with a cute guy. *This is, like, so weird,* she couldn't help thinking. *I'm so totally gone on Tyler, and I'm totally flirting with this stranger. It's like I've morphed into Sam or something.* Maybe Sam wasn't so bad, Jessica realized suddenly. Maybe he just enjoyed the game. After all, she was pretty sure that she was falling in love with Tyler, and here she was chatting it up with some guy she'd never seen before and would probably never see again.

Maybe Sam just . . .

Jessica clapped a hand over her mouth. Sam was outside on the pavement, smirking at her through the open door.

Busted! "Uh, listen, I have to get going," Jessica said uneasily. She moved away toward the back of the gallery, anxious to put as much distance between her and the guy as possible. She had a bad feeling she'd be hearing about this from Sam later.

I wasn't even doing anything! Jessica reassured herself. But somehow she had a feeling that Sam wouldn't see it quite the same way.

"Is that Cassiopeia?" Elizabeth asked, extending her hand toward the sky as she snuggled closer to Sam in the sleeping bag. The desert air was a little chilly at night, but that wasn't why she was wrapping herself around him.

He just feels so incredibly good. Elizabeth sighed in satisfaction. She loved the way his muscles felt beneath her hands, his whole body was incredibly sculpted, and she couldn't help wondering for the millionth time how a guy whose major activity was channel surfing got such an incredible build.

"This was such a great idea, Sam," she murmured, running her hands over his biceps. "I would never have thought of sleeping out, but you're right—it's ultraromantic."

"Hmmm." Sam nodded. "Can you believe how bright the stars are? I don't think that's Cassiopeia, by the way, but the Pleiades are over there."

"Do you think that was a coyote?" Elizabeth tensed. It sounded like an animal was howling, very far away.

171

"If it is, he won't disturb us." Sam turned his head so his mouth was inches away from hers. Elizabeth could feel his warm breath against her cheek.

"You mean you'll protect me?" she murmured, closing the distance between their mouths even further.

"Actually, I was going to say that the fire would frighten him away." Sam laughed softly.

"Oh, you!" Elizabeth hit his shoulder with the heel of her hand. "A lot of good you are. Besides, the fire's almost gone." She glanced toward the dying embers, where they'd toasted marshmallows over an hour ago.

"Well, anyway, we're safe here." Sam kissed her softly and then leaned back and studied the sky again. "I think that is Cassiopeia," he murmured. "I used to be really into astronomy when I was a kid, but I've forgotten a lot of it."

"Why's that?" Elizabeth trailed her hand along his chest.

"I got interested in other stuff." He paused for a moment. "Actually, my brother, Morgan, was majoring in philosophy in college, and he gave me his reading list. I got heavily into that for a while."

"And?" Elizabeth prompted. She was fascinated by what Sam was telling her. He almost *never* revealed anything about his family. She

172

propped herself up on one elbow and studied his face in the moonlight. "Go on—what happened then?"

"Yeah, well, my father didn't hang with Morgan being a philosophy major, so he made him switch to business." Sam's voice was flat. "So, no more reading lists, but I've always thought that I'd go on and . . ." He trailed off.

"Don't stop, Sam," Elizabeth said softly. "I want to hear this."

"I guess I always thought that I'd study philosophy myself in college, maybe even go on and get a Ph.D." He sounded hesitant, but even in the dark Elizabeth could see the way that his eyes were sparkling.

"Sam, that's so fabulous!" Elizabeth was excited. "I know you could do it too—you're one of the most brilliant guys I've ever met."

"Maybe." Sam shrugged. "I was thinking that maybe it was time I got a little serious, stopped slacking off. I don't know; maybe it's time for me to bag OCC."

"Of course it is!" Elizabeth sat up. She was thrilled that Sam was starting to take his academic career seriously. She'd meant it when she said that he was one of the most brilliant guys she knew, and she hated to see potential like his go to waste. "I mean, OCC is an *okay* school, but Sam, you could transfer to SVU!" Elizabeth pictured the two of them going off to classes together in the morning. Maybe they'd meet for lunch in the caf. *Maybe we could even move into our own house.* She imagined the two of them together without anyone else around.

"Oh, Sam, it'll be perfect!" She threw her arms around him.

"Huh? What will be perfect?" Sam asked. He sounded distinctly more subdued than she was. "First of all, who says I'd transfer to SVU? Second of all, where would I even get the money?"

"There's got to be some way," Elizabeth bubbled on, undeterred. "You could win scholarships, grant money. There's about a million ways that someone with your potential can work around the financial aspect."

"You're just, like, getting way ahead of things here." Sam disengaged himself from the tangle of her arms and rolled away slightly. "I said that I *might* be willing to bag OCC; I didn't say that I *definitely* was. I don't know what I'm going to be doing in the fall," he continued, sounding more and more irritated. "I'm just trying to figure things out. I don't want to get locked into anything yet."

I better back off, Elizabeth realized. She knew how much Sam valued his carefree existence, but she'd figured that he was open to making plans. *I*

174

guess he's just not ready, she thought as she reached to pull him back.

"Listen, Sam, we don't have to talk about this now," Elizabeth said quietly. "After all, there's a lot of more interesting things that we could be doing."

"That's for sure," Sam said. He was clearly still irritated, but the tension in his shoulders seemed to melt away as he gathered Elizabeth in his arms and kissed her deeply.

Why was I even bothering to stress on his education? Elizabeth wondered as she tightened her arms around his neck. *I can't believe I wanted to talk instead of kiss!*

She gave herself up to the sensation of the moment. It felt so amazing to be held so tightly and be kissed so thoroughly that Elizabeth couldn't help wondering what it would feel like to have even *more.*

"Sam," she whispered in his ear. "I really think I'm ready. . . ."

"Elizabeth," Sam groaned. "Don't you think that I want you too? But we have all summer—let's not rush things." He trailed kisses down the side of her throat. "This is so new, and I want you to trust me totally. I want to prove myself to you first."

"Mmmm," Elizabeth murmured. She felt too good to argue, but still she couldn't quite stop the little voice that was pricking at the back of her mind.

Why is it so easy for Sam to resist?

175

Chapter
Eleven

"I feel like I've been driving for, like, a hundred hours." Jessica groaned as she navigated the Jeep through the busy streets of Boulder. She tried to stretch her legs, which had stopped cramping about a hundred miles back, mainly because she'd lost all feeling in them. She could feel her nose getting burned in spite of repeated applications of SPF ten thousand, and if she were any hungrier, she'd faint.

Why did I think a road trip would be so fun anyway? she wondered. Of course, Tyler was turning out to be even more wonderful than she could have possibly imagined, but she could have lived without the permanent sun damage.

"Try two hundred." Tyler yawned as he tried to stretch his long legs out in front of him. There wasn't enough room in the front of the Jeep, though, and he wound up twisting himself into a pretzel. "I'm totally ready for a break."

"Well, we're stopping here, right?" Elizabeth asked from the backseat, where she and Sam had been dozing on and off for the past hour.

"I'm just trying to find Pearl Street." Jessica frowned. "It's supposed to be a pretty wild area, plus there's a really great mall."

"We're practically there." Tyler studied the map. "Take the next right, Jess."

"I hope that they have good burgers there," Sam said as he massaged the back of his neck. "Good burgers and plenty of brew. I feel like I've been sleeping on a box of rocks."

"I hope that they have clean bathrooms." Elizabeth tried to smooth the wrinkles out of her pink linen skirt.

"I just hope that they have somewhere to sit that isn't built like the front seat of a Jeep," Tyler chimed in.

"Well, looks like we're about to find out," Jessica said as she pulled into the parking lot.

"Hey, this looks way cool." Tyler perked up as he jumped out of the Jeep.

"You're not kidding." Sam bent to stretch the kinks out of his back. "This place is, like, hopping."

"You're right." Jessica looked around her with

a small smile. "Maybe it was worth driving forever just so we could end up here."

The pedestrian mall was crowded with throngs of college-age kids. People zoomed by them, blading, biking, and walking. Jessica even saw one guy juggling as he whizzed by them. Tantalizing aromas wafted out of the restaurants that were lined up. And as if that weren't enough, it was clear there were tons of great stores just waiting for her to hit them with her credit card.

"Omigosh!" Elizabeth exclaimed as she darted toward a large, colorful poster. "One of my favorite authors is lecturing here! I've got to go!"

Tyler studied a guidebook. "Jess, how about we hit the museum while Elizabeth and Sam hang out at the lecture?"

"Hmmm." Jessica considered for a minute. "Tell you what—I'll do the museum thing for a little while if we do the shopping thing for a long while first."

"I was figuring you'd come up with something like that." Tyler grinned. "Okay, you guys, I'm going to go and find out directions. Will you still be here when I get back?" He looked questioningly at Elizabeth and Sam.

"Actually, the lecture isn't for another hour," Elizabeth said. "And I'm feeling kind of hungry. I think I'm going to go grab us a couple of frozen yogurts. Do you want any?"

"No, thanks." Jessica shook her head.

"Me neither." Tyler flashed her a grin as he moved away. "Catch you guys back here in about twenty."

"Grab me a chocolate," Sam called after Elizabeth.

Elizabeth nodded and headed toward one of the many outdoor vendors, leaving Sam and Jessica alone together. Neither one of them said anything, and the silence lengthened uncomfortably between them.

Okay, so why am I all of a sudden stuck with Sam, and why does it feel so weird? Jessica wondered as she avoided his eyes. *I mean, okay, I think he's a pain in the butt, but I've lived with the guy for a year now. You'd think I would have something to say!*

Jessica had a strong idea why she was feeling so strange, though. She'd been feeling uncomfortable around Sam ever since he'd seen her flirting with that guy in the art gallery. She was sure that he was going to bust her for it, and probably when Tyler was standing right next to her.

"So, uh . . ." Sam cleared his throat. "You two are, like, really into the art thing, huh? I mean, you're off to a museum now, and I saw you in some gallery yesterday. . . ."

179

I knew it! Jessica glared at Sam. "Like I'm the only one that flirts?" she snapped. "Give me a break, Sam. I saw the way you were talking to that hotel clerk the other day. And what about the way you were staring at that waitress at the zoo?"

"Whoa." Sam held his hands up in front of him as if he could fend off Jessica's words. "Where did this come from? I was just trying to—"

"You were just trying to bust me because you feel guilty about the way you treat Elizabeth!" Jessica said wildly. "I mean, let's be honest here, Sam. You know I caught you twice already, but what about the times I'm not around? I don't like the way you treat my sister!"

"What waitress? What clerk?" Elizabeth said in a stricken voice.

Jessica and Sam whipped their heads around at the same time. Elizabeth was standing behind them, holding two dripping frozen-yogurt cones.

"What do you mean, he was checking out some waitress?" Elizabeth asked Jessica, a frown pleating her brow. "Sam, what's she talking about?"

"Uh, I—I gotta get out of here," Jessica stammered as Tyler walked up. "I'll catch you later, Lizzie." She pointedly ignored Sam as she ran to join Tyler.

*　　　*　　　*

Okay, someone wake me up and tell me I'm dreaming. Sam sighed miserably. *I signed up for a road trip, right? Not an express elevator to hell.*

Well, maybe he was being a little harsh, he reflected. The last few hours hadn't been hell, exactly, but they hadn't been a joyride either.

From the moment Jessica had fled with Tyler, Elizabeth had peppered him with anxious questions. She'd demanded to know what Jessica was talking about, and she hadn't stopped nagging him all the way to Illinois.

Nag, nag, nag, for the past two hundred miles! Just when Sam didn't think that he could take another second, they'd pulled into a diner to stop for dinner. Elizabeth wasn't nagging him over the dinner table, but she couldn't stop looking at him with those sad, puppy-dog eyes.

Things were going so well between us. Sam sighed as he dug into his chicken-fried steak. *Why'd she have to go and get all needy?*

Didn't Elizabeth get where he was coming from? Didn't she get that the more needy she got, the more she pushed him away? He wasn't a *bad* guy, but he was a *guy.* Sam figured that most other men were the same—put a noose around their neck, and they choked.

He glanced at her across the table, hoping that she'd be too busy with her salad to guilt him out

181

with one of her looks, but she was *still* staring at him with those huge, sad eyes! Boy, you'd think she'd found out that he had a wife and three kids or something!

I mean, yeah, I checked out a busty waitress, so? It happens; it'll probably happen again . . . , Sam thought as he looked at the waitress who was currently serving them. Her tight uniform strained across her ample chest as she reached across the table to clear Tyler's plate.

"Hey, what do you say we go and get some rooms?" Tyler wiped his mouth. "Let Sam settle up the bill while we go and find a place to crash." He gave Sam an understanding smile.

Sam nodded gratefully. Tyler was definitely pretty cool. He obviously could tell that Sam needed a break from Jessica and Elizabeth.

"Sounds good to me," Sam said, pushing back his chair. "I'll meet up with you guys in the parking lot."

He smiled at Elizabeth as she walked by him, but she didn't respond.

"Sheesh!" He ran a hand through his hair as he wandered over to the cash register. "What does she expect me to do, get down on my knees and beg for forgiveness?" The more he thought about it, the more he felt like running out the door and never looking back.

"But I really, really care about Liz." Sam sighed as he waited by the cash register. "I just can't stand the way she's hanging around my neck!"

"Your friends go and leave you all alone?" The pretty waitress who'd served them came up to take his check.

"Uh, yeah, kind of." Sam didn't feel like going into any long explanations.

"Yeah? How'd a girl manage to tear herself away from a good-looking guy like you?" The waitress smiled seductively.

Okay, moving into high gear. Sam blinked. What kind of a girl flirted that blatantly? he wondered. *Someone who isn't into heavy commitment,* he realized. The blood started to pound in his head. He wasn't going to rise to the bait. He really wasn't. After all, Elizabeth might be a pain in the ass, but he was practically in love with her. Not only that, but Elizabeth was drop-dead gorgeous. The waitress was cute, sure, but she couldn't compare to Elizabeth.

So why am I so into her all of a sudden? Sam wondered as he studied the small sprinkling of freckles across her nose.

He knew why he found the waitress so attractive. She represented freedom, and as much as Sam might love Elizabeth, he loved freedom more.

"So I'm about to take my break, go out back," the waitress continued. "Wanna join me? My name's Cathy, by the way. What's yours?"

My name's "already taken." And no, I don't want to join you—I've really got to go and meet my girlfriend, who I really, really care about. "Lead the way." Sam smiled. He followed Cathy out of the screen door at the back of the restaurant and into a little secluded garden.

"So you're new in town, huh?" Cathy sat down on a small wicker bench and patted the seat next to her.

"Yeah, how could you tell?" Sam asked miserably. He had no idea what he was doing, and he didn't know how he was going to get away.

"Because I already know every cute guy in town," Cathy drawled. She leaned forward, giving Sam a good view of her chest.

Sam couldn't help noticing how well built she was, and he moved over to join her on the seat.

"Yeah?" he asked. He couldn't think of anything more interesting to say, but that didn't seem to bother Cathy.

"Yeah." She nodded vigorously, causing her auburn ponytail to bob up and down. "You know what I'm wondering?" she asked.

"What?" Sam said. He was torn between wanting to stay and stare at Cathy's chest and wanting to tear out of there as fast as his feet would take him.

"I'm wondering if your mouth tastes as delicious as it looks," Cathy said in a sexy voice.

Okay, I really have to go now to meet my girlfriend, who I really care about. . . .

"Do you mind if I do a little experiment?" Cathy said. She bit her lower lip and looked unsure of herself.

"Uh, okay." Sam nodded. He decided that he must have stepped in some cement on the way out to the garden. That was the only reason he could think of for not running out of there as fast as possible.

"I'm going to see just *how* delicious it tastes." Cathy lunged for him.

"Mmm-hmm." Sam flailed his arms in the air for a second as his lips locked onto Cathy's. Finally he decided that the best place for them was around her waist, so he put them there.

Whoa, baby knows how to kiss, he couldn't help thinking as he squeezed her closer to him. He dimly remembered that he'd promised himself he wouldn't rise to her bait, but she tasted too delectable to think about anything else.

"Aaah!"

Guess she's, like, way into this too. Sam couldn't help feeling flattered. After all, he hadn't kissed anyone but Elizabeth for months, and it was nice to know that the Burgomeister hadn't lost his touch.

"Sam!"

Sam frowned a little as he deepened the kiss. That was weird. How could Cathy kiss him *and* talk at the same time? Was she a ventriloquist? Not only that, but she managed to sound just like Jessica too.

Jessica! Sam pulled away from Cathy in shock. He turned to see Jessica staring at him. She looked even more shocked than he did, and her face was turning an interesting shade of bright purple.

"Oh, man." Sam buried his head in his hands. "Oh, man," he repeated.

"Something wrong?" Cathy asked.

"That's one way of putting it," Sam said as Jessica ran away. "Or else you might just want to say that my life is in danger."

He closed his eyes and winced as he remembered the expression on Elizabeth's face when she'd heard that he'd just *looked* at another woman. Somehow he had a feeling that she'd take his *kissing* one even harder.

Sam didn't know what was worse—having to face Elizabeth after Jessica told her about what just went down or knowing that this time, Jessica was right about him treating Elizabeth badly.

Guess I'll find out soon enough, he thought grimly as he stood up and walked slowly out of the garden and toward the parking lot.

"I think it's probably safe to leave a lot of this stuff in the car overnight," Tyler said as he removed Jessica's hatbox from the back of the Jeep. "I mean, this is a pretty sleepy little town, and I don't see anyone planning a major heist of Jessica's beauty products."

"Hey." Elizabeth grinned at him. "You never know. I have a feeling that fancy Parisian skin care is in short supply here."

"You mean that weirdo special moisture mask that makes her look like an alien?" Tyler slung his duffel bag over his shoulder.

"How do you know about her moisture mask?" Elizabeth stared at him in amazement.

"I dunno." Tyler shrugged his broad shoulders. "She was smearing it all over her face the other night."

Jessica lets Tyler see her in that green goo? Elizabeth's jaw dropped. *Wow, that's a new one. She must really trust this guy. And I do too,* she realized suddenly. There was no denying that Tyler was a really great guy. Not only was he intelligent and mature, but he had a calmness that was a perfect foil for Jessica's high-voltage energy.

After standing by Jessica through a thousand boyfriend disasters, Elizabeth was really glad that Jessica had finally found the perfect guy for her. *I just wish that Jess could see that I've found the perfect guy too*, Elizabeth thought sadly. The things that Jessica had said about Sam came back to her in a rush.

Who was telling the truth? Sam or Jessica? Elizabeth didn't know who to believe. She wasn't sure that she *could* believe Sam, and she knew that she didn't *want* to believe Jessica.

I've got to stop stressing on this, she chastised herself. *I've got to focus on something else*. She reached to take out her backpack, but it was blocked by a thousand other things.

"Here, let me help you." Tyler moved some bundles out of the way.

"Thanks." She flashed Tyler a smile as he handed her the bright flowered bag that she kept her laptop in. "It's really great having you on the trip, Tyler," she said sincerely. "I'm glad that you and Jess are together."

"Hey, thanks for having me." Tyler shook his shaggy brown hair out of his eyes and smiled back at Elizabeth. "Not only am I getting a ride home, but I get to meet you."

"Yeah." Elizabeth laughed. She sat down on the curb, cradling her laptop on her knees. "I bet your summer wouldn't have been anywhere near as fab without trailing around after me and Sam." *And getting stuck in the middle of our problems,* she added silently.

"No, really," Tyler insisted, joining her on the curb. "You're such a huge part of Jessica's life. I'm really glad I got to spend so much time with the two of you. She really watches out for you, you know."

"Maybe a little too much," Elizabeth said ruefully, shaking her head. "She's really down on Sam."

"Like I said, that's because she watches out for you." Tyler's gray eyes shone with sincerity. "Look, I think she's being a little hard on the guy. So maybe he did check out that waitress—I don't know." He spread his hands out in front of him. "But I do see the way he looks at you, Elizabeth. Believe me, the guy's serious."

"Really?" Elizabeth asked, her face flushed a rosy pink. "I hope you're right," she said quietly. "I know that's the way *I* feel about him, but Jess kind of got me worried back there."

"Believe me, she's blowing the whole thing out of proportion." Tyler draped his arm around her shoulders in a friendly fashion. "Try not to take everything she says so seriously."

"Thanks for the advice," Elizabeth said. She

189

was struck once again by what a nice guy Tyler was turning out to be.

Jess has a great guy, she thought happily. *And no matter how much she tries to convince me otherwise—I do too.*

"I don't believe it; I just don't believe it," Jessica muttered under her breath as she ran toward the parking lot. "There's no way that creep is getting his slimy paws on my sister! Not if I have anything to say about it anyway!"

Jessica stopped to catch her breath. She wasn't sure whether she was so winded because she was running so fast or because Sam's truly outrageous behavior had taken her breath away.

"It's one thing to stare at some busty waitress." Jessica exhaled raggedly. "It's another thing to be all over them!"

"Jessica, hey, Jessica! Wait up!"

Jessica turned to see Sam running after her. "Talk about nerve. Well, all right, Mr. Burgess, let's see you talk your way out of this one!"

"Jess, give me a chance to explain." Sam grabbed hold of her arm. "I know it looks bad—"

"You are so wrong," Jessica hissed through clenched teeth. "It doesn't look bad; it looks *terrible.*"

"I'm sure." Sam was red in the face, but Jessica

couldn't tell if that was from running after her or from embarrassment.

He probably doesn't even have the grace to be embarrassed, she thought, her eyes shooting fiery sparks at him.

"Look, Jessica, I don't know what happened back there." Sam turned his head away, avoiding Jessica's glare.

"Oh, really?" Jessica's voice dripped venom. "Guess you were home sick the day they explained the birds and the bees, huh?"

"That isn't what I meant, and you know it," Sam growled.

"I guess *I'll* have to explain things to you." Jessica pointedly ignored Sam's outburst. Her voice changed and became sugary sweet. "Hmmm, let's see." She tapped her forehead, pretending to think. "What happened back there is that a certain two-timing toad who has his eye on every woman under the age of eighty finally went too far and is about to get seriously busted!"

"Did it ever occur to you that maybe you should just mind your own business?" Sam said through clenched teeth.

"This is my business!" Jessica shouted. She couldn't bear to look at him anymore. "Elizabeth *is* my business, you bastard! I happen to care about her more than you could ever imagine, and

191

I won't stand by and see her get hurt." Jessica whirled on her heel.

"Jessica!" Sam grabbed her by the arm. "Maybe if you kept your mouth shut once in a while, she wouldn't be hurting right now. Did you ever think of that?"

"You mean what Elizabeth doesn't know won't hurt her?" Jessica sneered.

"No!" Sam roared, his hands knotted into fists. "I mean that you take something perfectly innocent and twist it all out of proportion!"

"Groping some waitress does not count as innocent!" Jessica's voice was even louder than Sam's.

"Yeah, okay." Sam ran a hand through his hair in frustration. "I went too far, but I was *pushed*, Jessica!"

"Right." Jessica nodded. "I can see that. I *pushed* you into making out with that waitress. Makes perfect sense."

"I mean that you, you . . . look, I don't know *what* to say anymore!"

"Well, I still have plenty to say." Jessica stabbed a finger into his chest. "So listen up. Don't think for a second that I'm not going to spill to Elizabeth about this. Better go buy yourself some good shoes, Sam," Jessica raged on. "Because something tells me that when Elizabeth hears about this, you're going to be walking the rest of the way to Boston!"

Chapter Twelve

Elizabeth hummed a little tune as she stood before the mirror, unpacking her bag. She and Tyler had already checked in, and she wondered why Sam and Jessica were taking so long. "Oh, well, no biggie." Elizabeth went to the closet to hang up one of her flowered sundresses. "I just have more time to get ready for Sam, that's all."

Get ready for Sam . . . her gaze fell on the black lace nightgown that she'd already unpacked and laid on the bed. Elizabeth picked it up and held it against her body as she walked over to the mirror. "A little different than my baseball jersey." Elizabeth grinned as she studied her reflection. The nightgown gave her curves that she didn't know she had.

"Should I wear it tonight?" Her heart raced at the thought. *Should she?* Elizabeth was still feeling a little raw over everything that had gone down earlier in the day. Did Sam deserve to see her in the nightgown after all the things he'd done?

"But what did he do anyway?" She frowned. She knew that her sister didn't mean to hurt her, but she couldn't help wondering if Jessica's motivation had been to sour her on Sam. "After all, Tyler said that she was blowing things way out of proportion," Elizabeth reassured herself as she tossed the nightgown back on the bed. "And it's not like I haven't seen Jess overdramatize things before." Elizabeth nodded thoughtfully. "In fact . . . what's that noise?"

It sounded like a herd of wild elephants had broken loose and were stampeding down the hall. "It's either that or a crowd of drunken frat boys." Elizabeth grinned. The last time she'd heard a racket like that had been at one of the Sigma parties. The elephants stopped suddenly, but the noise was replaced by a frantic pounding on the door.

"What the . . ." Elizabeth strode to the door and yanked it open.

"Elizabeth!" Jessica stood in front of her. Her face was beet red, her hair was in total disarray, and she was holding on to the doorjamb for support.

"What happened?" Elizabeth was shocked. She grabbed Jessica by the wrist and yanked her into the room.

"Sa . . . Saam," Jessica managed to gasp between breaths.

"Sam?" *Omigod!* Elizabeth's first thought was that Jessica and Sam had been attacked in the parking lot and that Jessica had managed to get away while Sam was defending her.

"Just calm down, Jess." She led Jessica to a chair and rushed into the bathroom for a glass of water. *Please don't let there be anything wrong with Sam,* she begged.

"Here." Elizabeth dashed back to Jessica and handed her the water. "Take a couple of deep breaths, okay? Now, I want you to drink some water and tell me all about it."

"It was terrible, Liz." Jessica shuddered. She took a small sip of water and made a visible effort to calm down. "I've never seen anything like it."

"Like *what*?" Elizabeth bit her lip to keep from shouting. She was growing almost as frantic as Jessica was.

"Like Sam." Jessica put down the water and looked Elizabeth straight in the eyes. "Like the way he was . . ." She trailed off and buried her head in her hands. "Oh, I don't want to have to tell you this, Lizzie," she moaned.

"Tell me, already!" Elizabeth resisted the urge to shake Jessica by the shoulders.

"Okay." Jessica lifted her head. "I went back to

the restaurant to get Sam, only he wasn't inside. Someone there told me that they'd seen him go out back with that girl who was our waitress." Jessica paused for a second.

I don't want to hear this. Elizabeth got up and began pacing back and forth.

"So I went out back, and Liz, it was terrible. He had his hands all over her. They were kissing like they were—"

"Shut up!" Elizabeth clapped her hands over her ears. "I'm not going to listen to this crap, Jessica! You just have it in for Sam! Well, save your stories for someone else!" Elizabeth was shaking with rage; she couldn't remember the last time she'd been so angry at her sister. *Maybe never,* she realized with a start.

"I am not making this up!" Jessica exclaimed hotly as she jumped up out of the chair and began following Elizabeth around the room.

"Right!" Elizabeth wheeled around and stared at Jessica with her hands on her hips. "Tyler says that you're just blowing all of this way out of proportion. And I don't know, but somehow I have a sneaking feeling that Tyler's a little more objective about Sam than you are!"

"Elizabeth." Jessica seemed like she was about to cry. "You've got to believe me about this one. This is just too important to . . ." Her eyes fell on the nightgown spread out on the bed, and she stopped talking.

"Oh, no, Lizzie, you can't do this!"

"Can't do what?" Elizabeth snapped, her eyes following Jessica's.

"Tell me that nightgown doesn't mean what I think it does." Jessica passed a hand over her eyes to block out the sight. "Tell me you're not going to wear that as part of some big seduction scene." She collapsed on the bed and looked at the nightgown as if it were made of poison.

"What's it to you?" Elizabeth asked stiffly.

"Elizabeth," Jessica said firmly. "You can't do this. You can't throw away your life for a slacker like Sam."

"I am not throwing away my life!" Elizabeth yelled so loudly that the walls shook.

"Oh, no?" Jessica picked up the nightgown by one lacy strap and tossed it at Elizabeth. "Okay, so you're *not* going to turn down the offer from the University of London to stay in Sweet Valley, and you *weren't* planning on putting on this little number and seeing if you could lose your virginity tonight."

"None of this is any of your business," Elizabeth hissed as she bent to pick up the nightgown. For a brief second she wondered what it would feel like to strangle Jessica. She didn't think she'd ever felt so

197

angry with her before. *Or so distant from her either,* she thought sadly.

"That's where you're way off," Jessica continued. "This is totally my business, and you know it, Lizzie."

"Like I'm going to sit here and take advice from someone who threw their virginity away on a total jerk," Elizabeth sneered. She stopped, appalled at what she had just said. Elizabeth knew that Jessica was ashamed of her past mistakes, so why did she just throw them in her face? She braced herself for Jessica's next outburst.

"You're absolutely right, Elizabeth." Jessica's voice was deadly quiet. She spoke with an assurance that shook Elizabeth. "I have made some terrible mistakes, and that's why I want to stop you from doing the same exact thing."

"Red ball in the corner pocket," Sam announced as he chalked his cue. He lined up the cue and prepared to take the shot. The ball bounced off the table and landed on the floor with a thud. "Damn, I scratched," he announced unnecessarily as he moved away from the table to let Tyler take a shot.

"White ball in the center pocket." Tyler bent over the table.

No wonder I scratched, Sam thought as he looked down at his hands. They were shaking so badly, it was amazing that he'd even been able to hold his cue. They'd been shaking ever since Jessica had run out of the garden. Sam had followed her to the parking lot, expecting to see Elizabeth coming after him with an ax or at the very least in tears. But Elizabeth and Jessica were nowhere to be found. Only Tyler was there by himself, sorting through some bags. When he'd suggested to Sam that they go and play some pool and give the girls a chance to cool off, Sam had readily agreed.

Sam sighed loudly and reached for his beer. He couldn't help wishing that he were drinking cyanide instead. He had no idea what he was going to say to Elizabeth when he caught up with her. According to Tyler, she'd already gone to the room when Jessica burst into the parking lot, so he didn't know what, if anything, she knew.

Sure, like Jess didn't go running up to the room and spill everything. Sam shook his head in misery.

"Hey, stop beating yourself up." Tyler glanced at him sympathetically as he lined up his shot. "Look, I don't know what went down back there, but it can't be that bad."

Wanna bet? Sam twirled his cue between his hands, unsure of exactly how much he should tell Tyler. How much had *Jessica* told him anyway?

"Uh, so, um, what did Jess say, exactly?" Sam asked as casually as he could.

"She didn't say much," Tyler said as he easily sank his shot. "She just burst into the parking lot like a bat out of hell, yelling that she had to talk to Elizabeth. I told her that Elizabeth had already checked in, and she took off."

So Tyler's clueless. Sam looked at him. He'd been worried that Tyler was going to grill him, but Tyler seemed more interested in lining up his best shot.

"So what's going on anyway?" Tyler raised an eyebrow. He put down his cue and picked up his beer. "You and Elizabeth having problems?"

"I guess I'm just feeling really pressured," Sam said honestly. "Elizabeth's fantastic; that's not the problem, but she's just ultraserious. I mean, this whole trip thing is, like, putting our relationship on maximum warp. It's more than I'm into."

"Yeah, I know the name of that tune." Tyler nodded thoughtfully. "Look, the main thing is you have to be honest. It's not such a bad thing that you want to move more slowly than Elizabeth does. But you should let her know that."

"You're right," Sam agreed. He hefted his cue and walked back to the table. "But it's just not that easy. I mean, I'm into Elizabeth. I don't want to lose her."

"Listen." Tyler moved away from the table. "I'm just saying that things will be a lot better for both of you if she hears the deal from you instead of Jessica."

"Oh, man." Sam groaned. He put down his cue

and closed his eyes, imagining the scene that was probably taking place between Jessica and Elizabeth. He knew he should go and explain things, but he just couldn't bring himself to. When he thought about sitting down and apologizing to Elizabeth, he had the same feeling he had back when she first told him that she wanted to sleep with him. *I feel like a noose is tightening around my neck—I feel like I can't breathe!* Sam grabbed his beer and held on to it as if it were a lifeline.

"Jessica's convinced that you've been eyeing every waitress between LA and Illinois." Tyler scooped up a handful of pretzels. "I told her she was overreacting, but she's kind of hyper on the subject."

"Yeah." Sam took a deep breath. "You could say that again. She, uh, she kind of walked in on me and that waitress earlier."

"Really?" Tyler put down his cue and looked at Sam with a serious expression on his face. "Was anything going on?"

Yeah, the waitress was practically giving me artificial respiration. Sam avoided Tyler's eyes. "Um, well." He cleared his throat nervously. He didn't feel comfortable about lying to Tyler, but he sure didn't feel comfortable telling the truth. "We were talking, that's all. Maybe it was getting a little heavy. I think the waitress was into me, but so what? I wasn't into her."

"So you don't have anything to worry about."

Tyler shrugged. "I mean, so what if Jessica gets carried away and exaggerates things to Elizabeth? You can tell her the truth. Like I said, just be honest with her."

"Yeah." Sam nodded unenthusiastically. "I can tell her the truth," he said, his voice flat.

But somehow the thought of telling Elizabeth the truth didn't make him feel any better.

"I'm not going to listen to this anymore." Elizabeth glared at Jessica. "Look." She lowered her voice. "Maybe you really mean well. Maybe you're just looking out for me because of everything you've been through." Elizabeth reached out to take her hand. "I guess I should be thankful. But Jess." She paused and shook her head. "Sam isn't like the guy you lost your virginity to. He's different. He's a really good guy."

"Elizabeth." Jessica shook her head in exasperation. "You just don't get it. Sam *isn't* a good guy. He was busy fooling around with that waitress, and good guys *don't* fool around behind their girlfriend's back."

"Okay, fine." Elizabeth pulled away her hand as if she'd been stung. "Forget it. I'm going to go out and find Sam. I'm going to hear what he has to say about this." She grabbed her sweatshirt off the bed and slung it around her shoulders.

"Fine. I can't wait to hear this," Jessica said as she followed Elizabeth out into the hall. "I think that Tyler said he was going to hit the pool hall with Sam."

"Good," Elizabeth said over her shoulder as she raced down the stairs. She couldn't wait to find Sam. Jessica's accusations were still ringing in her ears. She had to find Sam as soon as possible so he could tell her that Jessica was wrong. *But what if Jess is right?* a tiny voice said in the back of Elizabeth's mind. *What if he really was making out with that waitress?*

She brushed the thought aside impatiently. She didn't want to act paranoid when she confronted Sam; she just wanted to hear his side of the story.

"So where is this pool hall?" Elizabeth asked grimly as she strode along the street.

"I think it's just a couple of blocks," Jessica panted as she raced to keep up with Elizabeth.

"This must be it." Elizabeth shoved open the swinging doors of the pool hall. She looked around the smoky room, searching for Sam and Tyler.

Sam. Her heart leaped into her throat at the sight of him. He was leaning against the far wall with a pool cue in his hand. *He looks incredibly sexy,* she thought as she made her way over to where he was standing.

Any woman would be thrilled to have him, Elizabeth told herself. The question was, would he be as thrilled to have any woman? *What if Jessica was right?* that tiny voice spoke up again. Elizabeth was suddenly nervous. *What will I do if he tells me that he was kissing another woman?* She swallowed hard as she stopped in front of Sam and regarded him warily.

"Sam," Elizabeth said quietly as she looked deep into his eyes, unsure of what she saw there.

"Elizabeth . . . I . . ." Sam started toward her, but he was stopped by Jessica, who stepped between the two of them like an avenging angel.

"Go ahead, Sam." Jessica spat out the words. "Tell Elizabeth what happened earlier. Tell her what you were doing when I walked in on you."

"Just let Sam talk." Elizabeth pushed her aside. "Sam? Is it true?" She looked away for a second and brushed her hand across her eyes.

"Is what true?" Sam asked briskly. "Is it true that Jessica is a pain in the ass who doesn't know when to mind her own business? Is it true that she blows everything out of proportion?"

That's what Tyler says, Elizabeth thought fleetingly. *That Jess blows everything out of proportion.* She looked back and forth between Jessica and Sam, trying to decide who was right.

"Sam," she began tentatively. "Just what exactly is there for Jess to blow out of proportion? I mean, you and the waitress weren't playing tiddledywinks back there, were you?"

"Elizabeth." Sam seemed to be struggling for words. "I don't know what kind of bull Jess is spilling, but I wasn't doing *anything.*"

"Then what did she see?" Elizabeth asked. Her heart thumped against her ribs. She wanted so much to believe Sam, but she just couldn't imagine that Jessica would lie. "What did she, Sam?" Elizabeth repeated more insistently.

"Look, I was asking the waitress if she could recommend a good place to crash. I mean, I thought that you guys might have a hard time finding a place. She told me that she was about to take her break and if I went out back with her, she'd, uh, I mean, she said she had a guidebook hidden somewhere, and she . . ."

"Oh, give me a break." Jessica rolled her eyes. "Are you trying to tell me you can't come up with anything better than that?"

"Uh, Jess?" Tyler cleared his throat. "Look, I think that Elizabeth and Sam have some stuff to work out between themselves." He stepped forward and put a hand on Jessica's shoulder as if he wanted to herd her out of the poolroom. "I think that we should give them a little space." He gave Elizabeth a sympathetic smile.

"Don't patronize me!" Jessica snapped, shrugging away Tyler's hand. "You're talking like you don't believe me!"

"I believe you're upset, Jess," Tyler said soothingly. "I believe you want the best for Elizabeth, but sometimes things get confused. And just for the record, Sam told me that nothing happened back there."

Elizabeth's heart lifted at his words, and she gave Sam a small smile, but Jessica didn't look happy at all.

"Okay, Tyler, I'm really glad to know that you trust me! Fine—hang with Sam if you want since you guys get along so well!" She pushed past them and ran out the door.

"Jessica, wait!" Tyler called out. When she didn't respond, he sprinted after her, leaving Elizabeth and Sam alone.

"Well, I guess we should head back to the hotel," Sam said. "Unless you want to shoot some pool." He gave her a crooked smile.

"No, I don't want to shoot any pool," Elizabeth said quietly. She wasn't sure exactly what she did want to do, but she followed Sam out of the pool hall and into the cool night air.

Sam draped an arm across her shoulders and smiled down at her, but Elizabeth felt too confused to smile back.

She was too busy trying to figure out why, when Sam had totally denied everything that Jessica accused him of, she felt worse than ever.

Chapter Thirteen

"C'mon, Liz." Sam sighed in frustration. "We've been through this, like, a million times already."

At least it sure feels that way, he thought as he regarded her tearstained face. They'd been replaying the same scene for the past hour, ever since they'd left the poolroom and returned to their hotel, in fact.

It's like we're in some never-ending loop. Sam rolled his eyes at the absurdity of it. First Elizabeth would demand to know if there was any truth to Jessica's accusations. Sam would earnestly deny them, and Elizabeth would be appeased for a while—like ten seconds. Then she'd get a little suspicious and start to cry. After a few minutes of that she'd dry her eyes and beg Sam to reassure her once again.

Hey, I can see why she's bumming, but the routine's

getting a little stale! Sam thought as he watched Elizabeth pace nervously around the room. *I mean, at this rate it would be easier just to confess!*

He shifted uncomfortably on the rock-hard mattress and eyed the TV longingly. A quick glance at his watch confirmed his worst suspicions: He was missing the Nick at Nite lineup of classic 'toons.

"Tell me again, Sam." Elizabeth pounced on the bed and looked deep into his eyes. "I mean, I just can't see how Jessica could be *that* confused. She must have seen *something* to get so upset."

Gee, why would she get upset? Hmmm, now, let's see—could it be because she's a world-class pain in the rear? Sam knew that he'd done Elizabeth wrong, but he couldn't help being ticked off with Jessica. Why *did* she have to go and tell Elizabeth everything? Didn't she understand that she was only hurting her sister? He realized that Elizabeth was waiting for an answer, and he took a deep breath.

"Hey, I don't know what's up with your sister. She's just, like, really overprotective," Sam said in as gentle a voice as he could manage. He was amazed that he didn't choke on the words.

"I know that she's just looking out for me," Elizabeth said anxiously as she twisted the ugly tan-and-orange bedspread. "And I know that she can sometimes overreact. But still, would she have told me that you had your hands all over that waitress if the two of you were just playing tiddledywinks?"

Score one for Elizabeth. Sam couldn't help being impressed by her logic. But why shouldn't he be? It wasn't as if Elizabeth was stupid; she was probably one of the smartest people that Sam had ever met. *That's why this story sounds so bogus.* He couldn't help thinking once again that it would be easier to tell her the truth.

Why don't I just spill and split? he wondered as he fell back against the pillows, worn out by Elizabeth's incessant questioning.

Sam didn't want to hurt Elizabeth, though, and he certainly didn't want to leave her. But it was getting increasingly difficult to remember why he wanted to be with her when she was acting like such a drag.

What had possessed him to go along on this road trip anyway? he thought as he listened to Elizabeth ask him about the waitress again. There had to be some reason he'd let himself in for this kind of torture.

I didn't just come along for the crappy meals and the lumpy mattresses, did I? He scratched his head. *And I sure didn't come along to hang with Jessica, did I?*

"Sam." Elizabeth prodded his shoulder.

209

"Come on, you seem like you're a million miles away! This is important! What really happened with that waitress back there?"

"I was just asking her advice about where we should stay," Sam said robotically.

"I want to believe you, but I have this terrible feeling." Elizabeth's beautiful blue-green eyes filled with tears, and Sam turned his head away so he wouldn't have to see them drip down her face. "I just have this terrible feeling that something's wrong," she repeated.

"Nothing's wrong," Sam said. He had to stifle the urge to grab one of the pillows and smother himself. *It's either me or Elizabeth,* he thought grimly. He felt like he was being smothered by her questions anyway. He felt worse than that. It was as if that noose around his neck was tightening by the second—and Elizabeth was the one doing the tightening.

She's strangling me! Sam thought in desperation. *Elizabeth and her crazy sister and all these commitments are strangling me!*

"I want things to be good between us," Elizabeth said earnestly. "And not just for my sake either. Sam." She reached for his hand. "It's really important to me that your parents see how well you're doing. That you've been able to make it without them. And Sam—" She paused for breath.

210

"Having a healthy relationship, that's like such a benchmark of maturity." She increased the pressure on his hand. "And I really want them to see how good we are together so they can respect you."

"What?" Sam's head was whirling. It wasn't so much Elizabeth's convoluted logic as the impact of her words.

His family. How could he have forgotten what was waiting for him at the end of this joyride?

Oh, man! Sam buried his head in his hands. *Obviously I'm being punished for committing murder in a past life! A needy girlfriend, a watchdog sister trailing my every move, a meeting with my family at the end of it—what's next? Nuclear war?*

"Saaam! Are you ignoring me?" Elizabeth wailed. "I want to talk about this some more!"

Sam turned white. Of course Elizabeth wanted to talk about it. She'd want to talk about it until she was blue in the face. She'd want to talk about it until he died of boredom.

"I'm outta here." Sam stood up abruptly, toppling the pillows to the floor. He studied Elizabeth's shocked face in the mirror as he walked over to the dresser and grabbed his sweatshirt. He couldn't stay there and listen to her for another second. He had to get out and get out fast.

"I'll see you later," Sam said as he slammed the

211

door behind him. He wondered if getting out was even worth it. After all, he knew that when he got back, he'd be subjected to yet another round of questioning.

"What the hell," Sam muttered as he charged down the stairs. "Maybe I'll get lucky. Maybe I'll get hit by a car."

Jessica kicked a stone out of her path with such savage force that it nearly broke the window of a nearby store. "Who cares?" she muttered as she slouched by, ducking her head low. She had more important things to stress about than a cracked plate-glass window.

"How could Tyler possibly think I was confused by what I saw?" Jessica raged as she slunk down the nearly empty street. She'd been wandering through the town ever since she'd run out of the pool hall.

At least he had the sense to run after me, she thought with a brief glimmer of satisfaction. It'd been a pleasure watching him grovel after he'd finally caught up with her. He'd been more than willing to apologize, but Jessica wasn't having any of it. She'd dismissed him and walked away with her nose in the air.

The only problem was that she had nowhere to go. If she went back to the hotel, she'd have to deal with Tyler again or, worse, Elizabeth, and Jessica was in no mood to speak to either of them.

"He must think I'm, like, a complete and total idiot! Does he think that I never saw anybody make out before? I'd have to be brain-dead or something to be confused by what I saw!" Jessica wasn't sure what was worse, having Tyler think she was a liar or having him think she was simply stupid.

"And what about Elizabeth? You'd think that after almost twenty years she'd trust me." Jessica collapsed against a stone wall and watched the cars go by. It was starting to get cold, and she was starting to get seriously bored. Not only that, but the stone wall was starting to get seriously hard.

"This is pretty beat." Jessica groaned as a few raindrops began drizzling down. "I better get out of here." She hunched her shoulders against the rain and started walking back in the direction of the hotel.

Hey, maybe I can hang here for a while, she thought as she passed by the little enclosed garden where she'd caught Sam kissing the waitress. She figured that it was probably empty. Most people had better things to do than hang outside in the rain. "Anything's better than going back to the hotel and facing the firing squad."

She poked her head through the opening in

213

the green latticework that shielded the garden from the street.

Her eyes practically popped out of her head at what was happening in front of her. *It's like déjà whatsit.* Jessica whistled to herself. *Either that or someone slipped something in my drink earlier!*

The garden wasn't empty. Sam was in there, and so was the waitress. And once again they had their hands all over each other.

As horrible as Jessica felt for Elizabeth, she couldn't help feeling vindicated too. Jessica made a rapid decision. This time she wasn't going to *tell* Elizabeth—this time she was going to *show* her.

She whirled around and raced off in the direction of the hotel as fast as her feet could possibly carry her.

"Elizabeth, Elizabeth!" Jessica gasped as she pounded on the door. Her lungs felt like they would burst. "Elizabeth, c'mon! Open up!"

The door swung open suddenly, and Jessica gasped at the sight Elizabeth made. She had thought she was shockproof after what she'd just witnessed in the garden, but what she was seeing now was in some ways even worse.

Jessica had been sure that Elizabeth would look like a mess. She'd pictured her opening the door with a tearstained face, wearing her old gray sleep shirt. Jessica would have been able to handle that.

She would have told Elizabeth to dry her eyes and get dressed, and then she would have dragged her off to see what Sam was up to.

Jessica could have handled that. She could have even handled *worse* than that. If Elizabeth had been hysterical, screaming and crying, she would still have known what to do. But right now, she was at a total loss.

Elizabeth looked *beautiful*. She was wearing her sexy black nightgown. It was sexier than anything Jessica had ever seen Elizabeth in. It was sexier than anything Jessica had ever seen *Jessica* in.

"Elizabeth! What's going on?" Jessica asked with a sinking feeling. She had a bad idea that she knew *exactly* what was going on. Elizabeth would never put on a getup like that unless she had serious seduction on her mind. She wouldn't drape herself in black lace unless she was . . .

She's planning to lose her virginity tonight, Jessica realized in shock. She pushed her way into the room and slammed the door behind her.

"Elizabeth! What's gotten into you?" Jessica spluttered.

"I'm really not in the mood for another scene right now, Jess," Elizabeth replied airily. She waltzed over to the dresser and, squinting into the mirror, began applying mascara.

Elizabeth's putting on makeup before going to

bed? Oh, no! Further proof, as if she needed any, that Elizabeth was planning on having sex with Sam.

"Elizabeth, you can't do this!" Jessica cried.

"Do what? Put on a little makeup?" Elizabeth looked over her shoulder at Jessica. "And just why can't I?"

"Don't play dumb with me!" Jessica said through clenched teeth. "I know what you're up to, and how you can even be thinking of doing it is beyond me!"

"Doing what?" Elizabeth was suddenly wary.

"C'mon, Elizabeth, this is me you're talking to. You can't tell me you just happened to throw that thing on." She gestured at the negligee. "You're thinking of sleeping with that creep. After everything that I've told you, you're actually thinking of sleeping with him!"

"Listen, Jessica." Elizabeth whirled around. Her face was flaming, and Jessica could tell that she'd struck a nerve. "Just what have you told me? Some wild hallucinations? Well, guess what? I thought that I wanted to sleep with Sam before, but thanks to you, now I'm sure."

"What do you mean?" Jessica demanded. "You mean that me telling you Sam's fooling around behind your back made you decide to go ahead and sleep with him? Oh, good one,

216

Elizabeth." Her voice dripped with sarcasm. "That makes a lot of sense. And here I was thinking that you were smart!" She collapsed on the bed.

"What I mean," Elizabeth said icily, "is that your wild accusations showed me how important it is for me to trust Sam. I need to show him that I believe in *him,* not in your crazy stories." She paused, and Jessica could see that she was blushing. "And I can't think of a better way to show him that than to make love with him."

Jessica gripped the edge of the bed. She was afraid that if she didn't, she'd strangle Elizabeth. Where did her sister get these half-baked ideas from? Jessica wondered. Wasn't Elizabeth supposed to be the sensible one?

"Okay, Elizabeth, have it your way," she finally managed to say through clenched teeth. "But just do me one favor first."

"What?" Elizabeth raised her eyebrows. "Listen to some more of your stories? Sorry, been there. Done that."

"No." Jessica shook her head. "You don't have to listen to me anymore." She got up off the bed and rifled through the closet. "Here." She tossed Elizabeth a pair of chinos and a polo shirt. "Put these on—we have a date with destiny."

"What?" Elizabeth caught the clothes and held

them against her chest.

"Get dressed," Jessica said tersely. "You may not want to listen to anything I have to say, Elizabeth, but you're going to look at something I want to show you." Jessica tapped her foot impatiently as she waited for Elizabeth to change.

"C'mon." She grabbed Elizabeth's hand the second she was dressed and dragged her out of the room. Maybe she couldn't *talk* Elizabeth out of losing her virginity, but she was pretty sure that after she showed her what was going on in the garden, Elizabeth would be burning that nightgown instead of wearing it.

How the hell did I end up here? Sam pulled away from the tight circle of Cathy's arms and shook his head in amazement. He didn't know how he'd ended up in the clinch with her. He really didn't.

He'd flung out of the hotel room in the worst temper, intending to walk around for a while and blow off some steam. But after wandering around the deserted streets for a few minutes, he'd found himself back at the pool hall with a cue in his hands. Tyler wasn't around, of course; he was busy with Jessica somewhere, but Sam figured that any of the guys hanging around the bar would be into shooting a few rounds with him.

The problem was that most of the guys seemed

to be laughing at him. Oh, it was nothing out-right. No one guffawed when he walked through the door, but Sam could see people nudging each other, and his face had flamed with embarrassment.

Clearly they'd all witnessed the earlier scene between him and the terrible twins. Sam could just imagine how that one looked. A big, burly guy getting chewed out by two little blondes. No wonder they were laughing at him. He threw down his cue in disgust and stomped out the door into Cathy's waiting arms.

It's not as if I planned this, he thought miserably. Cathy had just been there, walking by the pool hall. When she'd seen Sam, she'd hailed him like he was a long-lost childhood friend. *Well, not a friend, exactly.* Sam grinned ruefully. She'd coerced him back to the little garden and proceeded to give him a thorough lesson in mouth-to-mouth resuscitation. At least that's what it felt like, Sam thought. He pulled away from her, resisting the urge to wipe his mouth with the back of his hand. He didn't think he'd ever been kissed quite that way before. Cathy's embraces were so insistent that it was almost frightening. She acted like she was starved for male companionship. Sam wasn't a vain guy, and he knew that some women found him cute, but he couldn't help wondering if the only other men in town were monks.

She's, like, way into me. He brushed back his hair and studied Cathy underneath his lashes. There was no denying that she was pretty. He wasn't as sure about her personality; after all, she'd hardly said two words to him all night. He was also betting that she wasn't an intellectual firecracker à la Elizabeth Wakefield, but he didn't care.

Sure, Cathy isn't as beautiful as Elizabeth, or as smart, or as charming, Sam thought as he watched her reapply some lipstick. *But so what? Okay, she's missing all those things, but she's got something Elizabeth doesn't have—she's all about freedom. Elizabeth comes with some pretty heavy strings attached.*

"So, how long are you in town for?" Cathy snapped her lipstick shut and turned toward him with a dazzling smile.

"I dunno." Sam shrugged. "A day or two at the most."

"Yeah? Cool."

Sam was pleased that Cathy didn't seem to care that he'd be blowing out of town before she had a missile lock on him. He congratulated himself on being able to read her character so easily.

But hey, why shouldn't I be able to pick up on her vibe? Sam shrugged. *It's like looking in the mirror. Until Elizabeth, I never even thought about getting tied down.*

Sam didn't understand how he'd gotten tied down in the first place. In a way that was even weirder than the fact that he'd ended up here with Cathy. Hell, that was easy to understand in comparison. All Elizabeth had to do was pull the noose around his neck a little too tight, and he was happy to rush into the arms of any female who walked by. The real mystery was how had he let her get such a choke hold on him to begin with.

Well, that wasn't such a mystery either. Take a beautiful, intelligent, kind, and altogether wonderful girl like Elizabeth, and it was kind of hard *not* to let her under your skin. The only problem was that Sam didn't want *anyone* under his skin. He was into traveling light, and Elizabeth was heavy baggage.

Sam wanted to hang with who he wanted, do what he wanted, and not have to explain anything to anybody. He sighed heavily as he thought back to the scene at the hotel. Sometimes it seemed like being with Elizabeth was just one big explanation.

"What are you looking down about?" Cathy pouted. "You're not feeling bad about that blonde I saw you with, are you?"

"Nah." Sam shrugged. "I'm not stressing on her."

"That's good." Cathy nodded. "Because she's

not for you."

"Huh?" Sam swiveled his head and stared at her openmouthed. "How do you know?"

"I can just tell." Cathy gave a knowing smile. "She's got that wholesome thing going. Commitment, wedding bells, the whole nine yards. Stick with her and the most exciting thing that'll happen for you is picking out your silver pattern. You aren't into that. You're more like a free spirit."

"I sure am." Sam shuddered at the picture Cathy was painting. He reached out and grabbed her, crushing her to him with a force that surprised them both.

I sure am a free spirit! he thought as he lowered his mouth to hers.

Chapter
Fourteen

"I can't believe I'm letting you drag me around like this!" Elizabeth snapped furiously. As far as she was concerned, Jessica had lost her mind—there was simply no other explanation for the wild story that she was spinning this time. *Not only that, but I've lost it too,* Elizabeth thought. She was almost as mad at herself for going along with Jessica.

"At least one good thing will come of this," she panted as she tried to keep up with her sister. "At least Sam will be able to prove his innocence!"

"I'm telling you, Elizabeth," Jessica insisted as she pulled her along the empty streets. "He's not so innocent as all that! He was in the garden in back of the restaurant, and he was all over that waitress again!"

"If you were anyone else, I'd punch you for

saying that." Elizabeth glared at her. "I mean, really, Jess, what are you trying to pull here?"

"I'm trying to get you to see the light," Jessica explained slowly as if she were talking to a five-year-old. "I just don't want you making any stupid mistakes, Elizabeth."

"The only stupid mistake I made was following you out here without a jacket." Elizabeth yanked her hand away angrily. "It's freezing out here." She closed her eyes and imagined how much better she would have felt if she'd stayed in the hotel room. Sam would have come back, he would have seen her in the nightgown and taken her in his arms. . . .

"You're upset," Jessica said. She reached for Elizabeth's hand again. "Believe me, Elizabeth, I've been there. But trust me, a few tears are better now than a whole bucketful later."

"Jess," Elizabeth began carefully. She was torn between wanting to clobber her sister and being touched by her concern. "I know that you mean well, but don't you think I'm capable of making my own decisions?"

"Not about this, Elizabeth," Jessica said firmly. "Not without all the facts."

"Fine," Elizabeth said harshly. She was irritated again. "Just show me this, whatever you want, and then leave me alone, okay?"

"Okay." Jessica nodded. "Follow me, and Liz? Don't say I didn't warn you." Jessica led the way to the little enclosed garden at the back of the restaurant. She unlatched the gate that helped hide the garden from prying eyes and flung it open dramatically. "There!" she exclaimed triumphantly, gesturing with her hand. "What did I tell you? What do you see?"

"Oh." Elizabeth's face transformed. But instead of looking enraged or shocked, she looked touched. "Sam really is a lot like me underneath it all," she whispered.

"What do you mean?" Jessica hissed. "When was the last time you dragged a guy behind a restaurant and kissed him senseless?"

"Jess." Elizabeth tore her eyes away from Sam and looked at her sister with an expression of pity. "Take a look at what's going on."

Elizabeth moved aside, and Jessica looked into the small garden. Her mouth dropped open, and she rubbed her eyes for a second. "No!" she exclaimed. "It can't be!"

Sam was sitting by himself. There wasn't a busty waitress within a fifty-yard radius. He looked soulful and romantic, especially the way he was bent over a piece of paper, scribbling away. A lock of hair fell over his forehead, and he frowned in concentration.

"I know just how he feels." Elizabeth nodded. "Sometimes it's so hard to express yourself clearly. But I always feel so much better after writing in my journal. Obviously Sam feels the same way."

"I don't get it!" Jessica was indignant. "I saw him here with her. You've got to believe me, Elizabeth!"

"Oh, really?" Elizabeth closed the gate softly. She regarded her sister suspiciously. "What I believe is that for some reason you're trying to break me and Sam up. I don't know what your game is, Jessica, but I sure don't like it!"

"I . . . I was just . . . Liz!" Jessica sputtered wildly.

"You know . . ." Elizabeth tapped her lower lip thoughtfully. "I think I know what happened."

"You do?" Jessica said eagerly. "You mean you figured it out? Something happened between the time I ran to get you and now. She must have been called back off her break or something, right?" She whipped her head toward the restaurant, and sure enough, Cathy's busty form could be seen hard at work, scrubbing tables.

"No." Elizabeth shook her head decisively. "I don't think that's what went down here tonight."

"You mean you think that the manager caught them or something?" Jessica frowned.

"No!" Elizabeth stepped forward and poked

Jessica in the chest. "*This* is what I think happened. I think you're pissed off about not sleeping with Tyler. I think that you're so pissed off, you can't stand it that I'm going to be sleeping with Sam tonight, so you decided to ruin things between us!"

"Elizabeth!" Jessica gasped in shock. "That is so unfair! I would never do anything like that!"

"Oh, no?" Elizabeth looked unconvinced. "You mean, you would never stoop to being so petty? Seems to me I can remember quite a few times you've acted that way."

"But that was before!" Jessica protested. "I'm different now. You know how much I've changed, Lizzie!"

"Whatever." Elizabeth sounded extremely bored. She turned away and started walking back in the direction of the hotel. "I'm going back to my room to write in my journal, just like Sam is doing in his." She spun around and glared at Jessica. "It's a great way to work through whatever's bothering you. The next time you feel the urge to try and con me with one of your wild stories, I suggest you try it first," she finished icily as she stomped off down the street.

"This is probably the worst night of my life." Jessica groaned as she climbed the stairs of the

227

hotel. She felt limp and exhausted. She was completely worn out from her fight with Elizabeth. But that wasn't what was bothering her. In fact, Jessica would have gone head-to-head with her sister any number of times if she thought it would do some good. But she knew it wouldn't. Elizabeth was unbelievably stubborn, and when it came to Sam, she only believed what she wanted to.

"No, what's bothering me is the fact that Elizabeth is destroying her life because of that slacker!" Jessica paused, out of breath, on the fifth floor and considered the impact of her words.

Was Elizabeth really ruining her life? Maybe Jessica was being too melodramatic. "Let's see— what is Elizabeth really giving up for Sam? Hmmm. Number one." She ticked the items off on her fingers. "She's bailing on this University of London scholarship. Okay? Is that really that bad?" Jessica cocked her head. "Yeah, it's that bad. Okay, moving right along. Item number two. Elizabeth's going to lose her virginity to a guy who doesn't even care about her. Is it that bad?" Jessica started up the stairs again. "No, it's *much, much* worse!"

Jessica dashed down the hall with a renewed spurt of energy. Maybe Tyler could help her figure out what to do. Sure, they'd argued before, but Tyler was so incredibly fair-minded. When Jessica told him how desperate the situation was, he'd come around.

"Tyler!" Jessica burst into the room. "Tyler, we have to talk." She collapsed out of breath on the bed. "I seriously need your help."

"Really?" Tyler didn't seem very interested. He was seated at the desk, playing solitaire, and he barely glanced at Jessica as she lay gasping on the bed.

"Tyler, are you listening to me? Did you hear what I said?" Jessica sat up and looked at him in growing alarm. Tyler appeared to be completely oblivious to her, and Jessica wasn't sure she liked that. She'd never played second to a deck of cards before.

"Yeah, I heard you." Tyler nodded as he placed a red queen on a black king. "The question is, do I care?"

"Do you *care?*" Jessica repeated the words in disbelief. Where had her kind, considerate boyfriend disappeared to? "What do you mean, do you care?" she spat out. "I don't know if I like the sound of that, Tyler!"

"Well, I don't know if I like the sound of what you've been spouting lately," Tyler said easily. He swept the cards off the desk and began shuffling them in the palm of his hand. "If you want to tell me that you need my help because you have a problem, I'll be happy to help you." He got up and moved toward the bed. "If you want to tell me that you're hurting, I *really* care. But if you want to talk to me about Elizabeth and Sam, then Jessica, *I couldn't care less!*"

"But Tyler." Jessica sat bolt upright and grabbed his arm. "Don't you see? Elizabeth's problem *is* my problem."

"No, Jessica, that's where you're wrong," Tyler said gently. "Just because you and Elizabeth look exactly alike doesn't mean you're the same person. Her problems aren't yours."

"You don't understand," Jessica said stubbornly. "People who aren't identical twins *can't* understand. I just have to look out for Elizabeth. That's all there is to it."

"Okay, that's cool." Tyler joined her on the bed. "I can see why you'd want to look out for Elizabeth, identical twin or not. But Jess." He placed the cards carefully on the bedspread and took Jessica's hand. "You haven't just been looking out for Elizabeth. You've been watching her every step. Correction—" He gave her a lopsided smile. "You've been watching *Sam's* every step."

"But don't you see that he's bad for her?" Jessica wailed. "I mean really, really bad for her!"

"Oh, man." Tyler sighed. He let go of Jessica's hand and, picking up the cards again, leaned back against the pillows. "This is getting really old, Jess.

230

I mean, I've been hearing about this for the past six hundred miles. It was kind of interesting five hundred miles ago. It started getting stale four hundred miles ago, and terminal boredom set in about three hundred and fifty miles ago."

"I'm sorry if the things that matter to me bore you," Jessica said stiffly. She jumped up off the bed and walked over to the dresser. She picked up her brush and started yanking it through her hair.

"C'mon, Jess, don't give me attitude." Tyler began laying the cards out on the bed. "I've been listening to you bitch for a pretty long time without complaining. The least you could do is let me blow off some steam."

"Let's just forget it, okay?" Jessica pouted. She was barely listening to Tyler. Her mind was busy dreaming up plots to thwart Elizabeth's seduction plans. *There's got to be something I can do,* she thought, frowning. *I've come between Elizabeth and the best-laid plans often enough in the past. . . .*

"Listen, let's call a truce." Tyler got up off the bed and walked over to Jessica. He stood behind her and rested his head on top of hers. "I'm going to hit the shower, okay? Let's do something nice when I get out—take a moonlight walk or something." He squeezed her shoulders.

"Um." Jessica nodded. "Sounds good."

"See you in a bit." Tyler grabbed a towel from

231

the back of the bathroom door and closed it behind him.

Jessica bit her lip and stared at herself in the mirror. She had to come up with a plan and soon. Something Tyler said came floating back to her. *Just because you and Elizabeth look exactly alike doesn't mean . . .*

"Of course!" Jessica exclaimed. How many times in the past had she used the fact that she was an identical twin to her advantage? She'd impersonated Elizabeth at the bank, at school, and even with an ex-boyfriend.

"Well, now it's time to impersonate Elizabeth with another boyfriend," Jessica said to her reflection. She grabbed a rubber band and slicked back her hair into a ponytail à la Elizabeth. "What else?" She frowned. Her clothes would have to go if she was going to be convincing. She rummaged through her backpack, looking for the one pair of chinos and long-sleeved shirt that she'd brought with her in case it got cold.

"This better work," Jessica said grimly as she stepped into the chinos. "This just better work."

"I am so wiped," Elizabeth complained as she lay on her back, staring up at the ceiling. She'd been back at the hotel waiting for Sam for a while now, and she was getting tired and depressed.

It wasn't that she believed any of the things that Jessica had said about Sam, but it seriously bothered her that her sister and her boyfriend couldn't get along. She wasn't that happy about being alone either. She knew that Sam was probably still spooked about everything that had gone down earlier and that he probably still needed some time to write in his journal, but she wished that he could write in their room instead of hidden away in some secluded garden.

"Why do things have to be so complicated?" she whispered. "And why do I have to care so much?"

Elizabeth rolled over onto her side and got up off the bed. She'd had just about enough of lying around and feeling sorry for herself. "What can I do?" she murmured as she wandered over to the window and looked out. Maybe Sam was on the way back.

"No such luck." Elizabeth shook her head, staring down at the deserted streets. "Well, I'm not just going to lie around here waiting," she said as she paced back and forth. She remembered that there was a bar in the lobby of the hotel, and she decided that a drink wouldn't be the worst idea.

"I really need one," she said with a sigh. Well, that wasn't strictly true. What she really needed was a boyfriend who didn't have commitment issues, a sister who wasn't going ballistic, and a long, hot bath, but she'd settle for a drink.

"I'll have a lot better time down there than moping around the room," she told herself as she brushed her hair until it glistened and dabbed on some lip gloss.

Elizabeth bounded down the stairs with renewed energy. She pushed open the double doors of the taproom and walked over to the bar.

"Hey, buy you a drink?" a smooth voice said at her elbow.

Elizabeth turned and saw a slightly older-looking guy smiling at her over the rim of his glass. He was mildly cute or would have been if he didn't have such a slimy smile.

"Uh, no, thanks, I'm here with my boyfriend, actually."

"Sure, you are." He laughed. "I buy that. That's why you came in here all alone."

Oh, great. I just want to relax and hang by myself, not get hit on by some jerk who thinks that he has a really great line.

"So how about it, beautiful?" the guy persisted. "What's your pleasure?"

If there was one thing Elizabeth hated, it was being called *beautiful*. As far as she was concerned, it belonged in the garbage along with *babe* and *honey*. She stifled a sigh and looked around for an escape hatch. Guys like this one were a perfect argument for why she was in love with Sam. *He's pushy, rude, and sexist, and those are his good qualities!* She couldn't help grinning.

"Now, that's what I like to see. Do you have any idea how pretty you are when you smile like that?" The guy gave her a stupid grin.

"Hey," Elizabeth cried as she spotted a two-ton linebacker walking in the door. "My boyfriend just got here!" She pointed a slim finger at the new arrival.

"Hey, great meeting you—gotta run." The guy jumped up off the stool and ran away.

"Ha!" Elizabeth laughed as she ordered a beer. She was glad that she'd gotten rid of him so easily, but she couldn't help feeling a little lonely. Elizabeth took her glass and looked around the bar to see if there was anyone worth joining. She spotted a group of women clustered around a small table. They were obviously having a good time, and they didn't look like they'd mind a little extra company.

Elizabeth walked over and smiled at them. "You guys mind if I join you?" She raised an eyebrow. "The bar isn't the greatest place to hang."

"Sure—scoot over, Casey." A bubbly redhead grinned at Elizabeth. "I'm Hillary, and this is Angela, Casey, Nikki, and Brin. We ditched our husbands at the bowling alley and headed over here for a girls' night out. What's your story?"

"I'm staying at the hotel." Elizabeth sat down. "My boyfriend's out on a walk, and I got bored with waiting upstairs."

"Hey, another round," Hillary called out to a passing waiter. "Hmmm." She turned back to Elizabeth. "Somehow that sounds like you and he had an argument."

"No, really," Elizabeth protested. "We just . . ."

"Mmm-hmm." Angela nodded. "This lady's on the outs with her man. Well, don't worry, we'll set you straight. You know the best thing about a girls' night out?" She quirked an eyebrow at Elizabeth.

"No, what?" Elizabeth took a sip of her beer. She was glad that she'd joined their group. Their enthusiasm was contagious.

"The best thing," Brin said around a mouthful of potato chips, "the best thing is that after spending all evening together, we start to miss our husbands!"

"I know how you feel." Elizabeth smiled as she peeled off the label on her beer bottle. She was seriously starting to miss Sam.

"Ooh." Hillary gave Elizabeth an appraising look. "See that long face, ladies? This one is missing her man already. Get out of here," she said with a friendly smile. "Go back to him."

"Well, I don't know if he's back yet. . . ." Elizabeth trailed off uncertainly.

"So spend some time getting ready for him," Casey said suggestively.

"That's what I was in the middle of doing before," Elizabeth murmured. An image of the black lace nightgown flashed through her head, and she blushed. She buried her head in her drink, grateful that the dark lighting in the bar didn't reveal much. "I didn't get very far, though." She took a deep breath and decided to confide in them. "I think my boyfriend's commitmentphobic."

"Listen." Nikki hooted. "Take it from someone older and wiser. *Your* man isn't commitmentphobic. *All* men are commitmentphobic."

"The thing to do is show him how much you care." Angela nodded. "Men are really just scared little boys underneath it all, and they spook easily. Go back to your room," she urged. "Don't get all down because he's not proposing. Do your part. Set the scene."

That's just what I was thinking earlier—before Jess came in and ruined all my plans, Elizabeth realized. She looked around the table, nodding thoughtfully.

"You know what?" Elizabeth pushed back her chair. "You're right. That's a great idea, and you guys have been really great. Just what I needed to get my head on straight. I'm going to take your advice. Good night." She smiled at them as she walked out and into the lobby.

"What if Sam's already back?" She chewed her lower lip in disappointment. "If he is, I won't be able to set the scene." She wandered over to the bank of courtesy phones in the corner and held her breath as she dialed their room.

No answer. Elizabeth breathed a sigh of relief. Now she'd have plenty of time to get ready.

"But what should I do, exactly?" Elizabeth wondered. Just getting into her nightgown and waiting didn't seem that exciting. Her eye was caught by a small gift shop off on the other side of the lobby. The window displayed everything from beautiful candles to sewing kits to shampoo.

"Candles—that's an idea." Elizabeth closed her eyes for a second, imagining how the room would look bathed in the light of a dozen scented candles placed strategically around the bed. *Pretty romantic, not to mention the fact that candlelight's extra flattering*. She imagined how *she* would look draped in the nightgown with the flickering light playing over her skin. *Much better than that harsh overhead lighting*. She smiled as she walked into the shop.

Elizabeth quickly selected a handful of lilac-scented votives and moved over to the cosmetics section. She grabbed a bottle of her favorite bubble bath, added the matching lotion, and headed toward the cash register, her arms overflowing with her purchases.

"Anything else?" the salesclerk asked as she started ringing up the candles.

"No, I think that's everythi . . ." Elizabeth trailed off. She was suddenly aware of the display behind the counter.

Condoms. Dozens of them. *Millions* of them.

All wrapped up in bright little packages. Did she need anything else? Of course she did.

"Um, I'll have a . . . um." Elizabeth cleared her throat uncertainly. She was embarrassed that her voice was so high all of a sudden. What was the big deal? So she was buying a package of condoms. So what? She was a grown woman *and* she was in love.

"I'll have a package of condoms. That red box," she said hastily before the clerk could ask.

"Sure." The clerk seemed completely bored as she added the box to the pile of goods on the counter. "Is that all?"

"Yes." Elizabeth nodded decisively. Now she really did have everything she needed.

She paid for the items and grabbed the bag. Her heart was beating so fast that she felt like she'd just run a marathon.

"I can't believe I'm really doing this," she gasped as she ran up the stairs. "Let's see—what's the plan?" She ticked off the items on her fingers. "I'll take a bubble bath, get into the nightgown, and light all the candles. By that time Sam should be back. Is that everything?" She frowned. "There's something else I'm forgetting."

The condoms! Elizabeth giggled, and she ran up the rest of the stairs as if she had wings on her feet.

Chapter Fifteen

"Yuck." Jessica made a face at the reflection she saw in the mirror. "How does Elizabeth stand it?" she wondered as she took in the vision she made in her khaki-colored chinos and plain blue oxford shirt. She had to admit that Elizabeth's fashion sense had picked up a little this year, but still, for the most part she wore clothes like this.

"If Elizabeth only knew what a sacrifice I was making for her by wearing these clothes," Jessica grumbled as she plucked a tissue out of a box on the dresser and began scrubbing off her makeup. She winced as the rough tissues scraped her face, but she didn't dare go in the bathroom to wash her face. Tyler was still in there taking his shower, and Jessica didn't want him to see what she was doing. She had a sneaking suspicion that if he did know what she was up to, he'd tie her to the bedpost and wouldn't let her leave until Sam and Elizabeth were safely on their way to Boston. She was also pretty sure that Elizabeth wouldn't appreciate the sacrifice she was making by wearing chinos and kissing Sam.

Kissing Sam. Jessica shuddered as she tissued off the last of her makeup. The idea made her sick, but that's how far she was willing to go to make sure that Elizabeth didn't ruin her life. She stepped back from the mirror and nodded in satisfaction. She looked exactly like Elizabeth.

Perfect. Jessica smiled grimly. Nobody, not even Sam, would be able to tell her apart from Elizabeth, and that was exactly what she wanted. Because Jessica was about to try and pull the kind of stunt that only an identical twin could get away with.

She was going to *be* Elizabeth. She was going to wait for Sam outside the hotel and give him the kind of homecoming that he'd probably only dreamed about.

She was going to kiss him senseless, kiss him until his head was reeling from it. Jessica wiped her mouth in distaste at the thought. She wasn't looking forward to her task, but she was going to do it, and do it so that Elizabeth would see.

Because Jessica was sure that when Elizabeth saw how her boyfriend was carrying on with her

241

sister, she'd never talk to him again, much less give up her virginity to him *or* a scholarship for him.

Jessica just had to make sure that Sam had no idea who she was. Well, that was a no-brainer, she thought in satisfaction, swishing her Elizabeth-styled ponytail. The sticky part was going to be making Elizabeth believe that Sam had known that she was Jessica all along.

"Elizabeth knows that we can't stand each other." Jessica bit her lip, her mind working furiously. "She'll never believe that Sam went for me. . . . On the other hand, she'd never believe that I'd come on to Sam either." Jessica frowned as she ran over the possible scenarios in her mind. "Why am I even stressing on this?" Jessica's brow cleared. "Elizabeth will probably be so freaked out that she won't stop to think about things logically. She'll just see Sam for the creep he is, and things will be over between them."

Of course, Jessica herself wouldn't escape Elizabeth's wrath, but she'd weathered the storm before, and she was pretty sure that she could again. Besides, she and Elizabeth would have plenty of time to work things out on the drive back to Sweet Valley after they'd dropped off Tyler and dumped Sam by the roadside.

Jessica gave her ponytail a final flick with her brush and walked out of the room, closing the door softly behind her.

Her heart was thumping against her ribs and her palms were sweating uncomfortably as she bounced down the stairs. She walked out onto the hotel porch and leaned against the railing, looking up and down the street to see if she could catch a glimpse of Sam. The streets were empty, but Jessica didn't mind. That just gave her more time to prepare. She imagined what it would be like to kiss Sam. There was no denying that he was gorgeous, but that didn't make things any easier. Jessica swallowed hard and wiped her sweaty palms against her chinos. She was actually feeling more nervous than she wanted to admit.

What if things didn't work out? What if Sam saw right through her? Worse, what if Elizabeth accused her of seducing Sam?

"It doesn't matter," Jessica said fiercely. She knew what she had to do. She was going to make sure that her sister didn't throw her life away on a slacker like Sam. Sure, Elizabeth would be upset for a while, but after she got over it, she'd see that Jessica had done the right thing.

Jessica sighed heavily and braced herself against the railing as she waited for Sam to come slouching down the street.

Sam whistled a little tune as he walked down the street with his hands jammed in his pockets.

He was completely and totally exhausted, and he wondered if the date he'd made to meet Cathy later was such a good idea after all.

"Maybe she won't show." Sam shrugged. He'd hung out in back of the restaurant when she'd gone back inside and written her a little note suggesting that they meet later on. He'd been sure that a few more hours with her were just what the doctor ordered, but now he thought that a few hours with his pillow might be a better idea.

"I just hope that Elizabeth won't be waiting up to harass me." He groaned as he neared the hotel. "She's getting way . . . Elizabeth!" Sam was surprised to see her hanging over the porch railing with a bright smile on her face.

"Hey, what's up," he said warily. He braced himself for a torrent of questions. In spite of her smile, he had a bad feeling about what was about to go down.

"I've been missing you," Elizabeth said sweetly. She leaned even farther over the railing and looked deep into Sam's eyes, her own eyes twinkling with stars. "Where have you been?"

Here it comes. Sam tensed. "I, uh . . ." He trailed off. He couldn't think of an answer that didn't sound suspicious.

"I guess you just needed some time to cool off," Elizabeth continued in a sympathetic voice.

"I guess I was pretty hard on you, huh?"

"What?" Sam looked at her in amazement. He shook his head, unsure if he had heard her correctly. Wasn't she supposed to be screaming and crying? What happened to all the accusations she was supposed to be hurling at him? Sam scratched his head in confusion.

"Aren't you going to come up here?" Elizabeth asked seductively. "Or are you just going to stay there on the pavement, looking like a lost little boy?" She reached across the railing and grasped his hand.

"Uh, sure I'm coming up." Sam swallowed at the electric charge that was flowing out of Elizabeth's hand. His flesh tingled where she touched him. It was as if her whole body was on fire, and suddenly Sam wanted to get closer to that fire.

"Hey." He bounded up the stairs and onto the porch. "I missed you too." He gathered Elizabeth in a loose hug and kissed the top of her head.

"Can't you do any better than that?" Elizabeth purred. She tightened her arms around him and offered her mouth up to his.

"Elizabeth! What's gotten into you?" Sam asked in shock. Whatever else Elizabeth was about, serious PDA wasn't in her vocabulary.

"I told you." Her voice was as soft as silk as she rained little kisses down his neck. "I was missing you. I feel guilty that I gave you such a hard time before."

"Hey, give me a hard time whenever you feel like it if this is the way you make up." Sam shivered at the intensity of her caresses. In all the weeks that he'd been going out with Elizabeth, she'd never shown such passion before.

"I want you, Sam," she murmured against the hollow in his throat. "I want you badly."

"Elizabeth . . ." Sam was at a loss for words. He lowered his mouth to hers and kissed her deeply.

"Um." Elizabeth ran her hands through his hair. "Let's finish this upstairs, Sam."

Sam didn't bother to answer. He barely took his mouth from Elizabeth's as he kicked open the hotel door and made for the staircase.

"I don't know if I can wait until we get to our room, Sam," Elizabeth said as she came up for air. She began untucking his shirt and running her hands across his bare skin.

"Elizabeth!" Sam pulled away from her in embarrassment. He looked around to see if any of the hotel guests that were milling around the lobby were watching. "Whoa." Sam shook his head. He was a pretty casual guy, but even he didn't pull stunts like this that often. "Don't you think that we should wait just a little? I mean, at least until we're in our own hallway, if not our own room?"

"I don't know if I can make it—let's hurry," Elizabeth said, practically dragging him up the steps.

Sam wasn't complaining about the pace, though, as he followed her as fast as his legs could carry him. He couldn't get over the change in Elizabeth from just a few short hours before. What had happened to put her in this mood? But whatever had caused this sudden personality shift, he wasn't going to question it.

"I don't think I've ever felt this way before," Elizabeth said as they reached their floor. She stopped outside the door to their room and pushed Sam back against the wall.

"Um, now that we're here, don't you think we should just go inside?" Sam asked as Elizabeth pounced on him once more. He didn't relish the idea of being a sideshow for anyone who happened to walk by.

"But, Sam." Elizabeth practically growled his name. "I feel so wild tonight." She lunged against him, flattening him against the wall, and began kissing him even more wildly than before, if that was possible.

"Um, okay, whatever you say," Sam managed to choke out between kisses. He knew there was some reason that he didn't want to be making out in the hallway, but by the time Elizabeth had begun unbuttoning his shirt, he couldn't remember what it was.

Elizabeth giggled nervously as she stared at herself in the mirror. The black lace nightgown draped across her figure in a way that revealed curves she'd never suspected that she had. *And this time I'm not taking it off either,* she vowed. *No matter what insane story Jess cooks up.*

Elizabeth only hoped that Sam would be as impressed with the nightgown as she was. She gave her reflection a final glance before turning away from the mirror and gliding over to the bed.

Elizabeth started rummaging through the package she'd brought back from the gift shop. After all, it wasn't enough to just dress herself— she had to set the scene too. She grabbed several of the candles and scattered them in strategic places throughout the room. The exquisite lilac fragrance began wafting through the air, and she stood back and surveyed the effect that they made.

"Maybe it's a little too black magic." Elizabeth frowned, observing the flickering light that was casting eerie shadows against the wall. She wondered if she should blow a few of them out. She whirled back to look at herself in the mirror again. The candlelight transformed the nightgown from something that was merely sexy to something that was beyond stupendous. "Definitely black magic!" She grinned at her reflection. "The lighting's *way* too flattering to change!" She laughed, aware that she sounded just like Jessica.

Her breath caught in her throat as she realized that after tonight she and Jessica would be more alike than ever. After tonight they'd *both* be non-virgins.

Elizabeth would have never said that Jessica was more mature than she was, but there *was* a gulf that separated them. The fact that Jessica was more experienced with men had sometimes created a barrier between them. Well, that was about to change.

"I'm going to be making love tonight," Elizabeth whispered to her reflection. Her heart beat wildly against her ribs, and she felt so nervous suddenly that she had to sit down on the bed.

Something crunched underneath her leg, and Elizabeth looked down with a frown to see what she had sat on. *The condoms!* She pulled the box out from underneath her and held it carefully in her hands.

With shaking fingers she unwrapped the box and withdrew one of the foil-wrapped packages. She blushed slightly as she read the directions. They seemed so, well, so *intimate*. Of course she'd known that having sex was about as intimate as you could get, but she just hadn't realized it quite so *graphically*.

"I guess there's no going back after tonight," Elizabeth whispered to herself. She felt chilly suddenly, and she rubbed her clammy hands against her bare shoulders in an effort to warm herself.

She'd been so sure for weeks now that she wanted to make love with Sam. She was still sure that she wanted to, but now she was unsure about *herself*. Would she know what to do when the time came? What if she fumbled and made a fool of herself? She knew that Sam could be incredibly understanding, but she didn't want to do anything stupid at such an important moment.

At least she had set the scene correctly, she thought, nodding in satisfaction as she looked around the room. The candlelight cast a warm glow on everything, and the air was subtly perfumed. She smoothed down the covers on the bed and slipped the condom underneath the pillow.

Everything was ready. The only ingredient missing was Sam. Elizabeth wasn't worried that he'd be a no-show—she knew he'd just needed time to cool off. She was sure that he'd be along any minute. What *was* worrying her was all the noise out in the hall again.

Well, whatever it was, she wanted it to stop and

soon. Elizabeth got up off the bed and strode purposefully toward the door. "Whoever's out there's going to get it," she said grimly. She wondered if she was going to be confronted by a horde of frat boys swinging kegs of beer around, and she braced herself as she prepared to shout them down.

"Liz . . . oh, Liz, I can't believe what you're doing to me." Sam groaned against the silk of her hair as he came up for air. He was dimly aware that they were still in the hallway, and he wondered why Elizabeth didn't make a move toward their room, but he was too dazed to care very much.

"What's gotten into you?" he whispered as he trailed kisses along her delicate jaw. Elizabeth had always been passionate in the past, but right now she was just about reinventing the word.

"Why are you so surprised?" Elizabeth asked as she nipped his lower lip. "You know that I've been dying to make love to you for a long time now."

"Yeah, but . . ." Sam's answer was forever lost as he covered Elizabeth's mouth with his own.

"Oh, Sam, I've been waiting sooo long," Elizabeth purred as she finished unbuttoning his shirt. She slipped her hands underneath and began caressing his bare chest.

"You don't know how much I've wanted this

either," Sam said in a husky voice. "I've been holding off as long as I could, but it's been getting harder every day." He started in on the top button of her shirt.

That's strange. The part of his mind that was still capable of rational thought noticed that Elizabeth was wearing a pink-flowered bra. Didn't she have on a plain white one earlier? He couldn't ever remember seeing her wear a pink-flowered bra before.

Sam had more important things to think about, though, and he ran his hands over the incredibly smooth skin of Elizabeth's torso.

"Oh, Sam, you smell divine," Elizabeth said. "What's that cologne you're wearing? It's fabulous."

"Elizabeth." Sam pulled away from her with a small frown. "I'm starting to wonder if you really have lost it. You bought me this aftershave a week ago. Don't you remember?"

"Oh." Elizabeth looked nervous suddenly. "Um, sure, I remember. . . ." She raised her mouth to Sam's for another kiss.

Sam was more than willing to return the kiss, but there was a nervous prickling at the back of his mind. Something was off, and he wasn't certain what it was.

Why make a mountain out of a molehill, dude? Sam thought as he crushed Elizabeth even closer.

So she's acting really different all of a sudden. So what? So she changed her underwear? Who gives one? So she doesn't remember that she bought me a present—I can live with that.

But the feeling wouldn't go away, and the more Sam thought about it, the more things added up to . . .

"Oh my God!"

Sam whipped his head around. Elizabeth was standing in the doorway of their room, wearing nothing but black lace and a horrified expression.

"Oh my God!" Sam repeated Elizabeth's words unconsciously. He turned back to the woman he'd been kissing. "Jessica?" he hissed. He pushed her away as if she were carrying a deadly virus.

"Elizabeth." He turned toward her, his eyes filled with pain. But Elizabeth didn't even bother to look at him as she pushed him aside and sped down the stairs in her nightgown.

"Jessica?" Sam turned back to her in bewilderment. "Do you want to tell me what that was all about?" he snarled as he buttoned up his shirt. "Make it good too, huh? Because if you don't, I may just have to strangle you."

Chapter Sixteen

Elizabeth rushed down the halls so fast that she thought she might have a heart attack. That was fine with her, though, because her heart was about to split in two anyway. She knew that she shouldn't be running through the hotel in her nightgown. The logical thing to have done was to have slammed the door to the room and barricaded it so that Sam couldn't get in.

But Elizabeth couldn't bear to go back into the room that she'd set up so lovingly and with such great expectations just an hour before. She still couldn't believe what she'd seen. She was so convinced that she was having a nightmare that she had to pinch herself to make sure that she was awake. The pinch hurt, but it was nothing compared to the way she felt.

Elizabeth staggered through the lobby, which

was mercifully empty, and collapsed against the porch railing. She was shivering, and her teeth were chattering, but she barely noticed, she was crying so hard.

She'd known for a long time that Sam had "commitment issues," but that was a long way from betraying her so cruelly—and with Jessica! How could her own sister do such a thing? And Jessica was more than a sister—she was her twin, her *identical* twin, her best friend.

Elizabeth buried her head in her hands and sobbed quietly. What was she going to do now? How was she going to get over this? And what was she doing, standing half naked on a porch in the middle of nowhere?

This wasn't the way things were supposed to turn out, she cried softly. Right now she was supposed to be taking a long, luxurious bubble bath with Sam. She was supposed to be making love for the first time, not standing alone in the cold night air.

Elizabeth tried to block out the pain, but it kept coming in waves, each one stronger than the next. Every time she closed her eyes, she saw Jessica lip locked to Sam.

Not only was she hurting worse than she ever had before, but she was totally confused. Jessica hated Sam. What was she doing wrapped in his arms?

Have Sam and Jess been carrying on the whole time we've been on the road? Elizabeth wondered. No, it was impossible—they'd been at each other's throats practically the whole time, and Elizabeth didn't believe that anybody could be that great an actor.

Still, no matter how much they'd hated each other before, they'd clearly made up their differences. *And how.* Elizabeth began laughing hysterically.

She wanted to hate both of them, but she couldn't get past how betrayed she felt. Her hopes had been smashed beyond all repair, and she didn't know how she'd ever feel good again.

I was going to have breakfast with Jess too. Elizabeth rested her head against the porch railing. Her plan had been simple. Seduce Sam into a night of love that neither of them would ever forget, and then take Jessica out to breakfast and make up with her. She'd been so sure that everything was going to work out beautifully. Her night with Sam would have been magical, and telling Jessica about it the next morning would have been even more fun. Oh, not that she was planning to spill all the spicy details. But it just seemed to Elizabeth that after a lifetime of confiding in Jessica, the experience of losing her virginity wouldn't be complete without telling her sister. She could just imagine the way that Jessica would have laughed at her over their poached eggs.

"Guess that won't be happening now," Elizabeth murmured in a voice thick with tears. "I guess I won't be telling Jess anything for a long, long time." She sagged against the railing as she imagined the emptiness that stretched before her. "Guess I'm in for a long, lonely future," she whispered.

But she really had no idea *what* the future held. She only knew that in one night she had lost the two most important people in the world to her: her boyfriend and her sister.

And she was standing outside in the cold Illinois night, half naked with nowhere to go and no one to turn to.

Jessica wiped her mouth with the back of her hand as she gave Sam a look of pure contempt. She'd accomplished what she wanted, even beyond her wildest dreams. The look on Elizabeth's face as she dashed down the hall told Jessica everything she needed to know. Elizabeth wouldn't be talking to Sam anytime soon.

Of course she probably won't be talking to me anytime soon either, Jessica thought miserably. She winced as she imagined how bad Elizabeth must have felt when she saw her locked in Sam's arms. Jessica had to admit that Elizabeth had looked more shocked than she could have possibly predicted.

Had she hurt her too much? Jessica rubbed her temples, which were throbbing in pain. Maybe she'd underestimated her sister's feelings for Sam.

Sam. It was all his fault anyway, Jessica thought as she gave him a scathing look. If he hadn't been such a rat, she wouldn't have had to concoct such a painful scheme.

"Jessica," he spat out her name as if it were poison. "What the hell are you trying to pull?"

Jessica looked at him silently for a few moments. She couldn't believe that she'd actually spent the last twenty minutes kissing him. She never wanted to see him again.

"Get out of my way," she hissed as she pushed him aside and began running down the hall to her own room.

"Not so fast." Sam ran after her and grabbed her arm. "I want to know what just went down, Jessica, and I want to know now!" He gripped her arm so tightly that he left marks.

"Look, Sam, I'm not into talking about it." Jessica wrenched her arm away.

"Not into talking about it?" Sam raised his eyebrows and stared at her in disbelief. "C'mon, Jessica, even someone as mush brained as you has to know that isn't going to fly. You're going to tell me why you were just trying to bust my ass and break your sister's heart."

Jessica looked frantically up and down the hall in the hopes that some passerby would save her from Sam's probing questions. Unfortunately the hall was empty, and she knew from experience that if she tried to run away, he'd only run after her.

"Okay, Sam, you want the truth?" Jessica paused, her mind racing furiously. She had to come up with an explanation that would satisfy him, and she sure as hell wasn't going to tell him the truth. "The truth is," she said slowly, still formulating her excuse. "The truth is that I've always had this competition thing going with Elizabeth. I just had to prove to her that I could grab you." She glanced at him from underneath her eyelashes to see if he was taking the bait. It was hard to tell what he was thinking since his face was turning ten shades of purple, but she had a sinking feeling that he wasn't biting.

"No, really," Jessica persisted. "Not only that, but Elizabeth's always carrying on about what a great kisser you are." She practically choked on the words. "I had to see if she was telling the truth."

"Do I look like a complete and total idiot to you?" Sam asked in a slow, measured voice. His hands were clenched at his sides, and Jessica wondered if he was restraining himself from strangling her. "That has to be the stupidest sorry-ass excuse for a reason that I've ever heard. And take it from me—I've tried to pass off some pretty sorry excuses in my time." He ran a hand through his hair and shook his head in dismay. "You better tell me the real story, Jessica. I swear I'll get it out of you one way or another."

"All right," Jessica said quietly. She didn't know how Sam expected to get the story out of her, but she knew that she didn't want to stick around and find out. She'd have to come up with something more plausible. "The fact is that I was really pissed that Elizabeth and Tyler thought I was lying about you making out with that waitress." Jessica gave him a filthy look. "This was revenge."

"Yeah, okay." Sam shrugged. "Maybe I'm buying that. I don't know, but you're probably just stupid enough and mean-spirited enough to pull something that insane."

"Oh, don't act so high and mighty with me," Jessica snapped. "Let's not forget what drove me to this little stunt. You *were* kissing that waitress. Do you think I want my sister to lose her virginity to a creep like you? I *had* to do this."

"What do you know about Elizabeth wanting to lose her virginity?" Sam pounced on her.

"Like Elizabeth and I don't talk about everything," Jessica sneered. "And just for your information, she did *not* tell me that you were a great kisser."

"I am, like, so hurt." Sam rolled his eyes. "Like that isn't about ten thousand on the list of most

260

important things right now." He paused and looked deep into Jessica's eyes as if he could read the truth there.

"Okay," he said after a minute. "So you wanted to screw with Elizabeth's head a little for not believing you. And you wanted to make sure that I was out of the picture. Well, I'm betting that you accomplished that one." His tone was bitter.

"What do you care anyway?" Jessica said nastily. "If you cared so much, why *did* you have your hands all over that waitress? You couldn't care about Elizabeth and do that at the same time."

"You don't know what you're talking about." Sam's voice was deadly quiet. "My feelings about Elizabeth have nothing to do with what I did with that waitress."

"Oh, really?" Jessica raised her eyebrows, her voice dripping with sarcasm. "That's interesting. I'm glad that you don't let your feelings about Elizabeth get in the way of checking out every busty waitress between here and Timbuktu!"

"You just don't get it," Sam said through clenched teeth. "I care about Elizabeth more than you'll ever know. But having the two of you scrutinizing my every move is about as fun as having my toenails pulled out one by one." He paused and closed his eyes for a moment. "But if you think I'm going to stand here and talk about *my* relationship with Elizabeth, you've got another thing coming. Right now I'm more interested in *your* relationship with Elizabeth."

"How does my relationship with Elizabeth concern you?" Jessica asked. She tried to move off down the hall again. As far as she was concerned, the discussion was over.

"It concerns me deeply," Sam said quietly as he shot out his hand to grab her again. "Because even though you still don't get it, I really, *really* care about Elizabeth, and something tells me that after what went down tonight, I won't be seeing that much of her."

"So?" Jessica asked as she tried to jerk her arm away.

"So I'd like to know that she had you to turn to, even though I personally think that she'd be better off without you." Sam increased the pressure on her arm. "And something tells me that I'm not the only one that she won't be talking to after tonight."

"Of course Elizabeth will talk to me again." Jessica flinched at the words as if she'd been struck. "It might take her a few hours, okay," she amended at the look on Sam's face. "Maybe more like a few *days* to get over it. But she'll come around. She'll see that what I did was for the best." Jessica stuck out her chin defiantly.

"I don't think so, Jessica." Sam's voice was barely above a whisper. "Did you see the look on her face? She's hurting. Hurting deeply." He paused and turned his head away. "She's feeling betrayed, Jessica. That kind of hurt doesn't heal in a few days. Or even a few years. Something was severed between the two of you tonight. And you know what? As much as you've screwed up my life, I feel sorry for you. I lost a girlfriend. You lost a sister."

"Oh, come off it, Sam," Jessica scoffed, but something deep within her trembled at his words. "You don't know how it is between the two of us. She'll get over it, and we'll laugh all the way back to Sweet Valley." She finally managed to wrench her arm free, and she walked down the hallway to her room without even a backward glance, but she couldn't help feeling badly frightened.

What if Sam was right?

Sam walked slowly down the stairs. He felt like he had aged about a hundred years in the past hour. He couldn't remember the last time he'd been this tired, and he was sure that he'd never been as miserable before.

He paused at the entrance to the hotel and stared through the frosted-glass door to where Elizabeth was sitting by herself on the porch. Even from the back he could see how unhappy she looked. Her shoulders slumped forward as if she were carrying the weight of the world, and Sam

263

thought he could see teardrops splashing on the porch rail.

What have I done? Guilt sliced through him like a knife. He'd always thought of Elizabeth as proud and confident. Who was this broken woman?

"It's all my fault," Sam muttered. He'd never meant for something like this to happen. He hadn't wanted the relationship that Elizabeth had been pushing, but he sure hadn't wanted things to end up like this.

Well, to be fair, it was Jessica's fault too. *Jessica.* She was just lucky that he hadn't broken her neck. He didn't think that would have been too violent a reaction; after all, she'd practically ruined his life. . . .

Or had she? Sam stopped short with his hand on the doorknob. In his heart of hearts he knew that he and Elizabeth weren't meant to be. He'd been chomping at the bit for a while now. Elizabeth was into the couples thing. He was into hanging out and playing darts. Sure, he cared deeply about Elizabeth, but he didn't care for her ideas about relationships at all.

He realized that Jessica had given him an out. Did he want to take it? Sam wasn't sure, but he did know that he'd hurt Elizabeth badly. He had to talk to her. He had to apologize to her.

He pushed open the door and walked out on the porch. "Liz," he said uncertainly. "Talk to me, please."

Sam's heart nearly tore in half at the expression on Elizabeth's face when she turned around. She looked wounded, wounded and angry.

How could I have done this to her? he wondered. He knew then that his philosophy was right. You only hurt people when you got involved with them.

"Liz." He took a step toward her. She shivered and pressed herself against the railing as if she wanted to distance herself as much from him as possible. "I . . . I thought that she was you, Elizabeth. I mean, I thought that Jessica was you. She was waiting out here when I came home. She said she wanted to make up."

Elizabeth didn't say anything; she just continued to look at Sam with the same terrible look on her face.

"Look, Liz." Sam took a tentative step closer. "Didn't you see the way Jessica was dressed? She looked like you. How was I supposed to know?"

Sam watched the effect that his words had on Elizabeth. He was surprised to see that they soothed her. "It's true that Jess has pulled things like this before," she said thoughtfully. Her expression changed a little. Before she hadn't been just hurt; she'd been *angry* and hurt, but now the anger seemed to be fading.

She's going to let me off the hook, Sam realized. He wondered why that didn't make him happier.

She's going to let me off the hook, and I don't want her to.

Sam rocked back on his heels. He was stunned by the thoughts that were swirling through his head. He *did* want to take the out that Jessica had given him. He wanted to be free.

Elizabeth was standing silently. She looked like she was on the verge of making up her mind, and Sam saw that things could go either way. If he just gave her a little push to the wrong side, it would all be over. . . .

No more of Elizabeth's beautiful sunny smiles, no more of her brilliant conversation, no more of her caring about all of his troubles almost more than she cared about her own.

No more *his* caring about Elizabeth. No more holding her when she cried. No more talking to her about her hopes and dreams. No more kissing her . . .

No more nagging, no more neediness, no more strings . . .

"Elizabeth." Sam took a deep breath. "Wait. I'm . . . I'm not being honest here. I did know it was Jess. I mean, sure, I was fooled for a second, but I knew pretty quickly. Hey." He swallowed painfully, hating himself more by the second. "I always wondered what kind of a kisser she was anyway."

He stopped talking and waited to see what Elizabeth's next move would be. It didn't take long to see that he'd given her the push that she needed.

Her face paled completely, then turned a brilliant shade of red. She took a step toward Sam, her whole body trembling violently.

Sam stood completely still. He wasn't sure what he should do next. He watched Elizabeth as she raised her hand and . . .

Thwok! She slapped him across his face. Hard. Sam closed his eyes and nodded miserably. He should have seen that one coming. It was certainly no more than he deserved.

He heard Elizabeth push past him and run into the hotel lobby, and he let out a deep sigh.

He had done it. He and Elizabeth were finished. He was free.

Sam wanted to cry. He knew that was stupid; he'd gotten what he wanted, but that didn't stop him from feeling bad.

Elizabeth must really hate me, he thought as he walked slowly into the hotel. He wondered if she hated him as much as he hated himself, but he decided that wasn't possible.

Nobody could hate Sam as much as he hated himself at that moment.

Chapter Seventeen

"Elizabeth!" Jessica jumped up as she saw her sister walk slowly down the hall. She'd been sitting outside the door to Elizabeth's room for the past half hour. "Thank God you're back! I have to talk to you!"

Elizabeth didn't answer Jessica as she pushed past her into the room. She grabbed her duffel bag from under the bed and began throwing her clothes into it.

"Elizabeth!" Jessica dashed into the room after her. "What are you doing?"

"What does it look like?" Elizabeth snapped.

"It looks like you're getting out of here," Jessica said frantically. She swallowed against the rising panic in her throat. "You can't do that." She grasped Elizabeth's arm. "You have to listen to me!"

"Oh, I don't think I have to listen to you." Elizabeth whirled around and glared at Jessica.

Her voice dripped with venom. "I don't think I ever have to listen to you again."

"Elizabeth!" Jessica shrieked. "You don't understand what happened!"

"Hey, what's going on?" Tyler poked his head around the door, which both of them had forgotten to close. "You can hear you guys at the other end of the floor."

"Tyler!" Elizabeth pounced on him. "I'm glad you're here. You might like to know that your girlfriend here was just making out with Sam like it was going out of style."

"Jess?" Tyler turned toward her with a bewildered look on his face. "What's she talking about?"

Oh, no! Jessica buried her head in her hands. How come when she figured out her brilliant plan, she didn't stop to factor Tyler into the equation? Why hadn't she stopped to consider that one?

"Let's hear it, Jess." Elizabeth's voice was bitter. She crossed her arms over her chest and stared at Jessica. "I just decided that I wanted to hear your side of the story after all."

Jessica felt cornered. Both Tyler and Elizabeth were staring at her and waiting for an explanation. Elizabeth looked like she wanted to kill. Tyler mainly looked confused, as if he was waiting for Jessica to deny everything and set Elizabeth straight.

But what could she do? She *couldn't* tell them

the truth. If Elizabeth knew why Jessica had really been kissing Sam, that it was just to get him busted so Elizabeth would dump him, she'd be after him in a flash. She'd forgive him totally, and all Jessica's scheming would have been for nothing.

She'd have to use the excuse that she'd trotted out to Sam earlier. She'd tell them that she was pissed off because they didn't believe her and that she wanted to get back at them, so she put the moves on Sam. There was just one problem. If she told them that, then Tyler would dump her.

Jessica looked over at Tyler. Even with his dazed and confused expression, he was still totally gorgeous. *And totally wonderful in every other way,* she reminded herself. Could she stand to lose him?

Jessica didn't know what to do. She was aware that they were both waiting for her to say something, but she couldn't bring herself to say the words that would push Tyler away forever.

But I'll get over Tyler, she realized. Maybe it would take a while, and maybe she'd always regret it, but she would meet another guy someday. But Elizabeth . . . if Jessica didn't do the right thing by Elizabeth, not only would she lose a sister, but Elizabeth would go back to Sam and throw her whole life away.

"What can I say, Tyler?" Jessica shrugged. "I mean, yeah, I'm busted. The two of you pissed me off so much when you didn't believe me before that

I decided to get back at both of you by making a major play for Sam." She couldn't bring herself to look at Tyler, but she took a deep breath and plowed on. "I never meant to hurt anyone," she whispered.

"Jessica . . ." Tyler looked stunned. His reaction was even worse than Jessica had expected. He looked like he hated her, or at least like he never wanted to see her again.

Elizabeth wasn't saying anything. She just scooped some clothes up off the bed and walked into the bathroom. *I guess she wants to give us some privacy,* Jessica thought, relieved that at least her sister was taking things the right way.

"Tyler . . ." She took a step toward him, but he backed away from her as if she carried the plague.

"Leave me alone, Jessica." His voice was deadly quiet. "I'm going now. You can come back to the room in an hour after I've packed and left."

"Left?" Jessica turned even whiter than Tyler. "Tyler, you can't mean that you're leaving!"

"Oh, no? Let me tell you something, Jessica. This may sound really strange to you, but I don't like it when the girl I'm falling for decides to put the moves on some other guy. When you get back to Sweet Valley, don't bother to look me up."

"Tyler! Don't go!" Jessica grabbed ahold of him and tried to stop him, but he pushed her aside and walked out of the room. Jessica knew that it

271

would do no good to run after him. The tears ran freely down her face, and she wondered if she had done the right thing. "I just hope that Elizabeth appreciates the sacrifice I've made for her," she said, her voice thick with unshed tears.

"What was that, Jessica?" Elizabeth said as she walked out of the bathroom. She'd traded the nightgown for a pair of jeans and a baseball shirt. "I hope you and Tyler have made up," she continued as she slung her duffel bag over her shoulder. "Because even though I never want to see you again, I don't want Mom and Dad bitching that I left you all alone without the Jeep. I mean it, Jessica." She paused to check in her wallet for the keys. "You're not my sister anymore." She pushed Jessica aside and marched out the door.

"Elizabeth!" Jessica cried. She dashed out the hall and down the stairs after her sister. "Elizabeth, come back!" she yelled as she ran through the lobby and into the parking lot.

But Elizabeth was even faster than she was. She jumped into the Jeep without even a backward glance at Jessica and burned ten feet of rubber pulling out of the parking lot.

"Elizabeth!" Jessica called after the Jeep. But it was no use. She had lost Tyler, and she had lost Elizabeth.

*　　*　　*

Sam poked his head around the door cautiously. He wanted to make sure that the coast was clear before he went in and got his stuff. The last thing he needed was another emotional scene. He'd been skulking around the hall for the past twenty minutes, and he was pretty sure that he'd heard Jessica chasing Elizabeth down the stairs, but he didn't want to walk in on them if they were still in the room.

He breathed a huge sigh of relief when he saw that the room was empty, and he went in and closed the door quietly behind him. Sam looked around in surprise. He didn't know why, but he half expected the room to be trashed. It would have seemed fitting somehow. He'd imagined that when Elizabeth and Jessica had it out, the feathers really flew.

"Elizabeth's too mature to act out like that." He shook his head sadly. Elizabeth was more mature than all of them. She was certainly more grown up than he was—he couldn't even handle a real relationship. And as for Jessica, well . . . Sam shook his head. He had no idea what her game was.

He opened the closet doors and began throwing his clothes haphazardly into his duffel bag. The sooner he got out of the hotel, the sooner he could begin hitching a ride to Boston. Sam tossed the last sweater into the bag and went into the bathroom to check and see if he was forgetting anything. His aftershave was sitting on the edge of the sink, and he sighed heavily as he reached to grab it.

Elizabeth had bought it for him recently. He unscrewed the cap and inhaled the spicy scent. It seemed unbelievable that only a few weeks ago, he'd been so happy to be in a relationship with her. Sam tried to imagine what it would feel like to wake up the next morning without Elizabeth in his arms. Well, that was what he wanted, wasn't it? He wanted to be free, and he was.

"So why do I feel so awful?" he asked his reflection in the bathroom mirror. He considered tossing the aftershave since it had so many painful associations, but he shoved it into his duffel bag instead.

Sam looked around one last time before he walked out of the room. He wondered how things would have turned out if he hadn't kissed Jessica. Would he and Elizabeth be making love right now? Would he be holding her in his arms? Would he be slowly peeling that nightgown away from her satin skin? Sam closed his eyes against the images that flooded his brain. They simply hurt too much.

"Time to blow this joint." His voice was ragged with pain as he slammed the door behind him.

Sam trudged down the stairs, his heart almost as heavy as the duffel bag that was weighing him down with every step. He pushed open the doors that led to the porch and walked out into the deserted parking lot.

Not quite deserted after all, Sam thought as he saw Jessica crouched on the curb. Her head was buried in her hands, and Sam saw that her shoulders were heaving.

I can't believe what she did. He realized in a flash what exactly Jessica had done for her sister. Maybe she was wrong about how bad he was for Elizabeth, but she *had* acted with her sister's welfare in mind. She'd jeopardized her own relationship to save her sister from what she imagined was a fate worse than death. Sam couldn't even imagine loving someone so much. Would he ever sacrifice his own life like that for someone?

Well, he didn't have time to stress on that now. He had a wedding to get to and a long road ahead of him. He walked passed Jessica on his way to the interstate, getting ready to thumb a ride.

He stopped for a second in front of the curb where she sat sobbing. In spite of everything, he almost felt sorry for her.

"I hope it was worth it," he said softly. But Jessica didn't answer, and he didn't look back as he struck out for the highway.

Elizabeth pulled over to the side of the road as soon as she neared the entrance to the freeway. She was in no state of mind to merge in all that Chicago-bound traffic. Plus she'd wanted to put as much space as possible between her and her exes—boyfriend *and* sister—before she stopped for a break. She suddenly didn't know where to go: Boston was out, of course, and back to Sweet Valley? Forget it. She wanted no reminders of Sam or Jessica at the moment. Heading toward home wouldn't help at all.

"Of course, the moon wouldn't be far enough away." Elizabeth barked out a harsh laugh as she killed the engine and sat back in her seat.

She'd been driving on autopilot for over an hour, too focused on putting some distance between herself and Sam and Jessica to really think about everything that had happened. But as she sat by the side of the highway with nothing to distract her but an occasional passing car, everything came flooding back to her. She buried her face in her hands as if she could block out the memories of the past few hours, but unfortunately it wasn't that easy.

"How could Jessica have done it?" she wailed, her shoulders shaking with the force of her sobs. "How could Sam have done it?" Tears streamed down her face as the image of them locked in each other's embrace flashed before her eyes. They'd looked like they were glued together. They'd looked like they were deeply in love, or at least deeply in lust. Had she and Sam ever looked that right together? Elizabeth didn't think so.

"At least I found out what Sam was really like

before I made love with him." Elizabeth shuddered as she imagined what would have happened if she'd caught Jessica in Sam's arms *after* she'd lost her virginity.

"God, what a nightmare that would have been." Elizabeth sobbed even harder. She tried to stop, but the tears kept flowing. She reached for her purse and rummaged through it, looking for a tissue.

"What's this?" Her hand closed over an unfamiliar piece of paper. She pulled the paper out of her purse and flicked on the overhead light.

We wish to inform you that you have been accepted for the fall semester at the University of London. . . . Elizabeth squinted as she read the words out loud. She clutched the envelope in her hands. The reminder of what she had been willing to give up for Sam struck her with full force, and she shuddered in pain.

A tap at the window nearly made her jump out of her skin, and she turned her head sharply to see a cop standing beside the Jeep.

Elizabeth heaved a sigh of relief and rolled down the window. "Yes?" She sniffed. "Did I do something wrong?"

The cop stared at her for a long moment before speaking. "You okay, miss?" he said at last. "Did you have a breakdown?"

Yeah, I had a breakdown, all right, but not with my car, Elizabeth wanted to say. "No, Officer." She shook her head. "Could you tell me . . ." She paused,

277

her hands clenching the steering wheel. She had to remind herself to breathe. "Could you give me directions to the closest international airport?"

"Sure," the officer said. "That would be O'Hare. You want to get on the highway and follow the signs. You're not too far, and you can't miss it. Where are you headed?" he asked in a friendly voice.

"England," Elizabeth said tersely. She turned the key in the ignition.

"You got a long trip ahead of you," the cop said as he headed back to his car. "Are you going the whole way by yourself?"

"I sure am," Elizabeth said grimly. She floored the accelerator and turned on the highway. "I sure am."

Signs to the airport were everywhere. Elizabeth followed them blindly.

She glanced at the acceptance letter from the University of London. It lay on the passenger seat. Never had a piece of paper taken on such significance. Suddenly that piece of paper was the only thing holding her together.

London, England, was just about far enough away from Sam, her sister, and a betrayal she'd never forgive or forget.

The final exit for O'Hare International Airport loomed in front of her. Elizabeth took a deep breath, then sped along to the future awaiting her.

A future as far away from Sweet Valley as possible.

Check out the **all-new**.....

..... (Sweet Valley Web site—

www.sweetvalley.com

New Features

Cool Prizes

The ONLY official Web site!

Hot Links

.... (And much more!)

BFYR 202

You'll always remember your first love.

Love Stories

Looking for signs he's ready to fall in love?

Want the guy's point of view?

Then you should check out *Love Stories*. Romantic stories that tell it like it is—why he doesn't call, how to ask him out, when to say good-bye.

Love Stories

Available wherever books are sold.

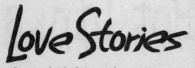

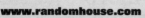